# Karen's Secret

# Karen's Secret

## SUSAN KAY BOX BRUNNER

Published by FWB Pubications, Columbus, Ohio

Published in the United States of America
ISBN: 978-1-940609-76-8
Fiction/Romance/Contemporary
16.05.12

To my son, Mark, without whom life will
never be quite the same. Peace.

# ACKNOWLEDGMENTS

The author wishes to acknowledge the following people for helping bring this book to light: Beth Loughner, author of five books, Mandy Larger, librarian, -Dustin Lewis, photographer, and Christie Burke-Crawford, for her unwavering support. A heartfelt thank you.

# 1

Karen Day was lost in past and present thoughts when, looking up at her parents' house, she parked her car. Sliding out from the burnt orange Barracuda vehicle, Karen caught the smell of the honeysuckle bushes lining the old, crumbled driveway. She noticed the full bloom on the rose of Sharon. Soon they would cascade into double bleeding hearts. Yes, it surely was a picture-perfect, manicured yard.

A sudden pounding noise got her attention. Karen turned so quickly it caused her free-flowing hair to do a complete 360-degree circle. She saw a short, beefy man adjusting his silk tie. She knew it must be Nathan Drum, the realtor, for his work truck was parked in the neighbor's driveway. His advertisement of "Homes Be Sold" were widely known. Standing beside him was a "For Sale" sign in her parents' front yard.

Putting her hands on her hips and taking a deep breath, she joined Nathan for one last look at the home and grounds where she had grown up. Karen paused on the steps, visualizing her mother and father sitting in their rocking chairs. They would be rocking in synchronized time, going back and forth, sipping on their freshly brewed iced tea. She could almost hear them talk. She listened for a familiar squeak going up the front steps. It did not let her down. Willing her emotions down, she tried to push the tears to suppression.

Nathan seemed to understand this challenge before her. She could see his eyes following her as if he could see the mixed emotions run across her face and red-rimmed eyes.

Going through each of the now-empty rooms caused her to reckon with deep inner feelings. Coming across the "much-used" fireplace brought back a lot of memories. One of them was of the stockings and their purpose of hanging on the stone mantel the night before Christmas. Each stocking had its own name, date, and birth year sown on it. The bedrooms were all empty and swept clean. There was not a spider or a web to be found. Her mother's sewing room had recently become just a vacant room. There was not even a scrap of material or a spool of thread left behind.

Slowly, she moved down the hall. Seeing the office space her dad had once used and sitting in his oversize chair became sobering. She glanced at the floor. Rising from the chair, Karen noticed a picture on the floor. Kneeling, she grasped a black-and-white portrait. It was of herself at around four years of age. In a flashback, she saw it sitting on her father's desk in a silver-tone frame. Memories chased her from the room, and she made her way to the back door to gain a lung full of air. A sigh escaped.

Walking the grounds only served up more memories. She thought of the turkeys her mother used to raise. Looking to the right, she saw the old red barn. During the winter season, the zoo allowed horses to be boarded out with special families. The memories brought back the tender loving care her father gave them. All their personality and life had appeared and now became just a vague, but not empty, impression.

There was something left she needed to do—a parting look in the basement, for it held a secret. The secret lay beneath a big three-foot round cement storm plug as it did during her childhood. Its viewing glass was built into the top.

Her footsteps failed when Nathan came back into view as he was quickly tromping her way. It was company she didn't need.

Karen said, "Nathan you go ahead and lock up. I will pull the door closed behind me when I leave." Snorting, he reluctantly agreed while placing the padlock on the front door.

She waited until his taillights disappeared before opening the heavy oak basement door. She gripped onto the thin, worn rail that lead to the dark basement. The steps were way too narrow and steep. As she was carefully walking down them step by step and holding on to the rail, a huge shadow appeared in front of her. It jumped and something bumped her right leg. Karen covered her mouth, holding in the scream, and stood ever so still. Feeling her throbbing heart, she tried to speak but nothing came out. Clearing her throat and finally mustering a sound, she stomped her foot, hit her hand on the stairway wall, and demanded, "Who goes there?"

Seeing only the gigantic whites of its eyes, Karen looked up the stairway and found a raccoon staring back. As if in slow motion, it rose on its hind feet but decided not to hiss. Panic had set in. Karen was still gasping for air as it slowly turned. She noticed the colors were a grayish brown with a white-ringed, bushy tail as the light trailed from the doorway at the top of the stairs. Hearing the pitter-patter of feet scampering out the front door was encouraging. After pausing, she continued down the basement steps, forcing her breathing to remain under control.

There was nothing left in the basement except the natural light still filtering dimly through the window and a toss pillow from upstairs lying on the cold, dry floor. Looking around, she shook her head at the odd shape of the walls and floor where the huge inserted storm plug lay. Karen debated at the thought of using the pillow to kneel on while looking down through the viewing glass on the round cemented storm plug. It was profusely covered with layers of dust and dirt, making her view impaired. She couldn't see anything at all. Karen let out a disappointed sigh. Looking would have to wait for another time.

As Karen stood, she promised the house out loud, "I will come back again and see your secret lying beneath the big storm plug."

Gazing around once again, she noticed a burnt-out little light over the white, sterile walls and neatly painted gray battleship floor. Nothing had really changed.

Sad and lonely were the facts facing Karen. She had lost track of time. The sun was setting in the west, and darkness was all around her as the moon went under a cloudy covering. Shuddering, she pulled the house door closed; and as the final episode ended, a feeling of a not-too-far fall wind breezed past her.

Upon exiting, she definitely felt a chill in the air. Karen rolled up the car window while traveling. The radio was playing "Night and Day" by Frank Sinatra, but all she could hear was her stomach growling. It sounded like an off-pitch flute with its own sound of a musical symphony. The growling kept repeating itself again and again until raw pain set in; Karen realized she had not eaten. While stopping at a red light, she saw a restaurant to the right. It had a massive, flashing neon sign that said "Eat Here." She quickly put on her turn signal and parked in the lot. Rummaging through her purse, she found one, two, three, no, four quarters, seven dimes, four nickels, and then a lone dollar. Karen knew a call was necessary for the intention to let someone know she was fine, but eating came first.

Flipping through her little red phone book, she found Sara's number. Thinking of Sara brought a chuckle to her mind. They had forever been the best of friends. One would begin a sentence and the other would finish it. The pay phone metal felt cold to her fingers as she dialed in Sara's numbers by memory. She touched the "penny swear necklace." Karen had never taken it off since they had exchanged them in high school many years ago. Perhaps it was childish, but all the same, she had worn it with pride.

Sara came on the line. "The room is here for you presently to crash for the night. Ken is out of town for the evening on some bank business Jud had sent him on. I took Timmy over to his grandma's for the night. She had been asking for him to stay. So it's just us girls tonight."

Karen smiled. "Thanks I'll be right there."

She knew it would be the perfect place to just chill out and do some serious thinking about the mess her life was in and hopefully find some answers. Karen knew Sara had plenty of questions, but she knew Sara, out of respect, would not ask anything until she was ready to mention things or unless the subject was brought to the surface.

As Karen turned into the asphalt driveway, Sara flashed a charming, magnetic smile, the kind that warmed the heart. She motioned Karen to enter the organized one-car garage.

Sara said, "You need to park in here for the night just in case it rains. I don't want to be responsible for the artistic paint work on the car should the weather turn bad."

Their eyes met in question, but Sara's eyes were especially piercing and very brown and seemed to reach the private part of your soul. They gave each other a friendly hug before walking toward the spare bedroom. Karen, being only too gratified and much exhausted, accepted the welcome stay for the night. Karen let her eyes peruse the room, a smile forming on her lips. It was a very attractive room, painted in a very easy-to-the-eye country blue. It was a complete style designed by Sara; Karen had helped her although the style was not her taste. Exhaustion settled over her body like a cloud. What she wouldn't do for a moment of tranquility, a moment to shut her eyes. She sank on to the bed and waved Sara on.

"Give me just a few minutes. Then we will catch up."

Sara smiled and backed from the room. Karen heard her say, "Sweet dreams." She floated out of consciousness as a peaceful sleep descended.

In the middle of the night, Karen woke up in a sweat. Where was she? Blurry eyes scanned the room. She was in Sara's place! She sank back in to the bed.

Feeling thirsty, she went quietly to get a drink of water. She pulled a chair up to the cabinet and, stepping up, reached for a small blue drinking glass. She felt the bed beckoning. But sleep did not come. Like a fleeting summer storm, it evaded her. She punched her pillow. Her mind felt like it would explode. Thoughts about Jud, her husband, and being anchored in this loveless marriage were unbearable. He scarcely talked with her anymore. Just to be in his arms was also a thing of the past. Karen sensed he was no longer interested in her.

Her mind kept playing the scene of just several weeks ago—she had acknowledged the news from Jud's statement about his parents getting a divorce and how devastating it was for him to face.

For the first time since their marriage, Karen saw tears forming in his eyes as he explained, "I thought my parents were a solid team."

"What happened?"

The words nearly chocked him.

His face had showed the hollowness of grief where once happiness used to grace the eyes. A sadness lured deep within.

Jud had been blindsided, pure and simple. His parents had planned a divorce while he was still in college. Time was on his side for a while, but the news and deed finally came. Karen considered this devastating—even the main reason for being shut out of his life. When he needed her the most, he refused her comfort and care. He didn't want to face the overwhelming possibilities or the parents' reasoning.

Tom and Joan Day had invested a lot of money in stocks and bonds. Their returns paid off well. During one of their many travels, both found they did not share many of the same interests with each other. Tom retired as a CPO from his bank, and Joan retired from writing famous jingles for a crackers company. The vice president, Eli Jones, worked jointly with Joan for a number of years. They had grown devoted to each other. She and Tom finally separated, and not long afterward, it led to a full-blown divorce.

Society did not approve of divorce in those days; it just wasn't acceptable. People of all walks of life looked down on those who were divorced, and society shunned most people involved with a divorcée.

Now, Karen's parents were also retired. Her mother had sold a thriving turkey business, and because the leases of her father's breakfast bars were expired, he closed out their industry and sold the equipment. Her parents decided to travel, taking a world cruise by booking one or more countries at a time.

As Karen lay on the bed, thoughts for her best friend Sara's wedding came to mind. It had been wonderful. Sara had been so busy planning for her special day. The couple was married at the Corner Church, quite an appropriate name since it rested on the quiet corner of First and Main. It was a humble white-painted building with a tall steeple. The church was known for performing weddings only, and a cone-shaped bell rang happily after all ceremonies.

The treasured people attending the wedding were Sara's mom, Louise; dad, Paul Weekly; Ken's dad, Jon; and his mother, Sylvia News. Also gracing them with their presence were a handful of Ken's and Sara's closest friends. Jud and Karen were to stand as witnesses at the front of the church.

The bride's mother wore a simple street-length pink dress while carrying a hand-stitched hankie. Her father arrived in a wheel chair, wearing a plain business suit of gray cotton.

Sara redesigned a form-fitting wedding dress made out of taffeta material she had received from a friend at a vintage shop. The dress, she had been told, was originally worn in a high school play. It looked like a picture featured in a bridal magazine: simple but breathtaking. The bodice was form-fitting while the skirt was A-line in shape. The headdress was of white netting, which displayed an understated taffeta bow.

Ken wore a three-piece gray pin-striped business suit with a white single-ruffled long sleeve shirt featuring polished-gold cuff links. My, he had looked devilishly handsome.

Looking like a storybook bride, Sara carried long stem white roses with baby's breath mingled in. The arrangement was surrounded by dainty pink puritan white satin ribbons gather at the base of the flowers.

Karen's mom, Mrs. Kate Page, helped Louise with the intimate reception dinner for the wedding party, family, and a few friends. Louise had rented a side room at one of the leading hotels in town—with the help of Kate, for she had secretly given money to Louise. Both ladies were excellent cooks. The meal was elegant yet conservative. Everyone marveled at the taste of the chicken casseroles and ham with scalloped potatoes dishes.

Karen pondered for a moment about Ken's gift of organization. In his office, pens and pencils stood in a stainless steel container. He could tell if anyone had moved even one pen out of its place. In his briefcase, labels were used for placing everything, and nothing was ever misfiled.

He had bought a house for Sara and him to live in after they were married. He had made the purchase earlier in the year and had Sara especially design each room.

Karen began thinking more about her friend and things Sara shared about Ken when they dated and how she felt. Remembering brought a smile to Karen's lips as she looked up to the ceiling fan. She recalled one of the weekly reading groups led by Jack Nite that the three of them attended. As they were leaving her house, Jud, Karen, and Sara heard the phone ring. Sara got so thrilled upon finding out it was Ken.

He said, "I will meet you at the group meeting tonight, but most likely I will be running late."

Karen recalled how airless Sara seemed.

Jud had mentioned that Ken had been working on an exceptional project, causing him to spend a tremendous amount of time at the bank.

"Karen, my heart did a cartwheel when I heard from him," Sara sputtered. "He means the whole world to me!"

The reading group's study topic had been on history. Karen remembered how Sara had nudged her and whispered, "I'm not staying focused."

Finally, it was over. As the group dispersed to leave, Sara mentioned, "I'm staying behind so Ken and I can talk. He'll be taking me home."

Karen assured Sara with a slight nod and gave her arm a squeeze as she turned to leave with Jud and some of the others from group. Karen brought to mind why Jud had taken her home. They both had an early day at work the next morning with her doing hair appointments and him seeing banking clients. Jud always went to bed with the chickens and got up with the rooster. In her mind it made him seem so steady, so reliable. A smile broke on Karen's face.

# 2

Sara's hand reached for a pencil and then grabbed the paisley-covered diary from her nightstand. She sat Indian-style on the bed and closed her eyes. She wanted to pen everything about Ken exactly the way she remembered, not leaving one glorious thought to be forgotten. Karen would want to know everything.

Sara began to write.

> Dear diary,
>
> Oh yes, Ken caught me looking at him, and I turned beet red. I could feel the heat beginning at the base of my neck and continuing to my face. All I could do was stare at him. Our eyes locked as if I were being pulled onto an outgoing wave into the ocean. He's so dead gorgeous! His complexion is fine-looking. His skin tone is pure milky white and so smooth. It was all I could do to keep my hands off his smooth, square jaw. He has the most beautifully long, onyx hair with waves like the morning tide. It just shined. I am so into him. Shameful, I know.

Sara let a girlish giggle slip. She poised her pen to write again.

> Making matters worse, he flashed me his award-winning smile. His teeth are perfectly straight and so white

as if they have been bleached. I couldn't help noticing a deep dimple on the left side of his cheek. I'm truly glad I sat down because my stomach was tied into knots. He almost made me forget the surroundings and my reason for being there.

Then he walked over rather slowly, looking cool, calm, and composed. It was just the opposite for me. We locked eyes again, and I knew he was definitely attracted to only me.

The only other time I've ever had this much passion within my soul was during one of my home design projects. Then I have lots of opinions and drive. I think this aggressive drive is what has made my career successful. Good night, dear Diary. See you again. Sara.

It was a beautiful morning with big fluffy clouds and the sun was shinning brightly. Sara pranced about like a princess straightening up the house, her mind brightly focused on Ken. Oh, a person didn't have the right to feel so happy.

The phone rang as she cast the dust rag across the end table.

"Well, hi, Ken," Sara said breathlessly. What's up?"

"Sara, may I come over in an hour? We need to talk."

"Sure." She bit her lip at the seriousness of his tone. "I'll be here. We can sit on the front porch swing, if that's okay."

> Dear diary, I'm on pins and needles. Ken and I have been dating for a couple of months and his voice sounded unusual. I don't know if it's good or bad. I must let Karen know. I'll pen later. Sara.

Ken took Sara's hand as they sat on the swing and he sweetly began. "I spoke with your father, and he agreed it was all right for me to court you." He gave her a crooked smile. "I wanted to know if you would be in agreement to date just me and to be mine?"

A little timid but deliriously happy, she nodded. He reached over and, ever so gently, gave her a kiss. She could feel his nervousness as he placed a promise pin on her sweater.

He said, "Will a three-month courtship be enough?"

Smitten, she made eye contact. "Yes." Reaching for his face, she offered up her lips to seal their time frame of dating. She secretly hoped he would pop the big question of marriage at the end of their arrangement.

Sara dropped the dish rag in the suds and shut off the hot water to listen. The phone rang again, and she sprang into action.

"Hey, Karen," Sara greeted breathlessly. "I was going to call you this morning! What's up?"

There was hesitation. "Do you have time to talk?"

"Sure I do!"

"What's going on with you?"

Sara stretched the phone cord into the kitchen as she poured herself a glass of milk. Leaning by the stool in the kitchen, she replied, "Ken asked me to be his girl! He wanted me to commit for a three-month period of courtship. Then we will review if there is a next level with us or not."

"Wow. What did you say?"

"Of course, I said yes. Karen, I wished he would have asked me today to marry him. I know he's the one."

"I'm happy for you. I really am. I hope it works out for both of you. Sara, I need to go or I'll be late getting to work. Talk with you soon or call me."

As the lines disconnected between them, Sara hesitated and felt doubt about Karen's lack of enthusiasm for her. She thought Karen was almost sarcastic. Sara, being taken back, nodded her head, wondering if her friend was overworked or if she was having a problem with Jud. She made a metal note that she would pray and speak with Karen later.

Time seemed to flash forward all too fast for Karen. She dealt with her new hair clients at the salon, doing perms or giving specialized colors, while Jud again was in his busy season, up to his eyeballs in his work at the bank. She hated being this busy and isolated. She hadn't seen or talked to Ken and Sara much over the past three months. When Sara called again, it took Karen a little off guard.

"Hi, friend."

"What's up, Sara?" While waiting for Sara to reply, she heard that familiar swish and squeak of Sara's favorite chair. She guessed Sara must have flopped down.

"Karen," Sara begun, "you're not going to believe this, but Ken called me right after he went home the other night. He said in his low sexy voice that he wanted me to go with him to the burger shop the next afternoon."

"Sounds interesting. So what did you tell him?"

Sara let out a playful grunt. "I said yes, of course. He came over and we walked to the burger place." She stopped a moment. "We held hands along the way, and our talking was so comfortable. Karen, it reminded me of the way you are with Jud."

Karen felt the need to respond, but the words stuck fast in her throat. "Sara, I'm glad for you." There was a long pause. "But you need to think about the long term. These feelings might pass or fade. Nothing lasts forever."

Over the phone line came a slow ho-hum before Sara said, "Did you get up on the wrong side of the bed, Karen, or what?"

Karen was in a state of despair, and a long disgusted sigh came across as Karen spoke again. "Go ahead. Tell me about your joy."

"First of all, friend, what's really going on with you? Why are you so down in the dumps? Did Jud forget to bring home flowers or take out the trash?"

Wavering, Karen felt it was wrong to discuss her unhinging relationship with Jud, so she yawned. "I'm just not sleeping very well at night. It's the old, used lumpy mattress. Sorry. Now what were you saying?"

"Well, sparks of electricity transferred through Ken and me as we were holding hands. Karen, I felt it, and Ken was reluctant to release my hand. It was like he wanted our moment to last forever. I know I sure did."

Through all the dilly-dallying, Sara asked, "Why don't I come over? I want to show you what Ken gave me. Is now a good time?"

"Sara, my time is all yours. Just overlook my lack of wow factor."

Her doorbell chimed, and Karen went to open the door for Sara. She set a tall glass of iced tea on the coffee table, and Sara immediately took it. After a few sips, Sara exclaimed, "It's been an amazing day."

Karen sat down in a slump. "How is your mom and dad doing?"

Sara looked puzzled for a moment but eased back into the sofa. "Oh, okay. Mom's been taking care of Dad. He's been in a lot of pain from that old injury. It's hard for him to get up at times. He's using the wheelchair more and more." She stopped for a moment and reached for a Kleenex. "It's hard to watch sometimes."

"I know," Karen agreed.

Immediately, Sara sat up. "Enough of this depressing talk. Let me tell you about Ken."

For the next fifteen minutes, Sara spoke of nothing but Ken's attributes.

Karen mustered a smile on her face as Sara prattled on, regretting the knowledge that she had once felt like Sara. It was imperative to show her supportiveness even though things were more than strained between her and Jud. But hearing the happiness in Sara's voice as she talked about Ken was tough to hear.

Looking at Sara, Karen could see how deeply taken Sara really was with Ken. She just glowed. When she talked, it was with a free spirit and lightheartedness. Karen wished she could be more like her right now.

Suddenly there was a haunted silence, and Karen noticed Sara's waiting expression.

"What did you say, Sara?"

"Where were you? You seemed miles away."

A smile was plastered on Karen's face while trying to sound normal. "Oh, you'll understand some day. Do you want another glass of tea?"

"Yes. As I said before, your iced tea is the best!"

With relief, Karen slipped out to the kitchen and brought back the pitcher.

Sara took a long sip and smiled. "I noticed Ken at the restaurant kept putting his hand in the left pant's pocket." She patted her pocket. "I saw an outline shape of a square box there. He just kept fidgeting with it. I felt he was ready to officially ask me to be his wife." She looked at Karen. "Did you know about my ring? Had Jud or Ken said anything to you?"

"No, I hadn't heard a thing. Did he have it?"

"Yes! Yes, he did! Oh, he makes me feel special all the time. You know he had proposed marriage to me just two weeks before, but not with giving me a ring." Dreamily, Sara continued. "Our afternoon slipped into evening. It was perfect. The slow gentle wind was blowing, and it was just right for me to wear a sweater."

Karen rubbed her arms. "I would have put on a jacket. I think this weather is cold."

Sara looked at Karen in query as she went on. "Oh, quit kidding me." Walking over to the window, Sara took a deep breath "The moon was peaking full with the stars hanging heavily sprinkled throughout the heaven."

Karen couldn't keep the sarcasm out of her voice. "I know, I know! One could almost reached out and touch them, right?"

Sara shook her head while remaining full of life. "The night was clear and the air was so pure." Motioning to her ear, she smiled. "You could hear the crickets as they chirped. It was beautiful, just stunning. Then, Karen, Ken brought out the pink velvety box, and he finally presented the ring. Karen, he was so sweet as he pledged his undying love for me."

Sara spoke about sitting on the restaurant bench for a long time. And how he placed the ring on her finger. How tears spilled down her face. How he wanted to know what was wrong.

Karen could feel pain building within her chest as Sara went on and on!

"Karen, it was amazing to touch to his face and let him know how much he was loved.

Sitting across from Sara, Karen touched Sara's knee. "Aren't you the happy one now."

Sara splayed her hand out and flashed her shiny diamond. "He leaned into me and honestly told me that he felt like my touch had burned him like a branding iron."

"This is getting too deep. Do I need my boots?" Karen remarked.

Sara looked confused for a moment yet beamed. "Gradually, he lowered his head and carefully dropped me a warm, passionate kiss, and it caused me to shake uncontrollably to the core. Ken bent again to touch my willing lips, but I reached for his hair and brought his head down for our lips to meet. Karen, it's a mutual agreement we were in the 'now and forever' stage. I thought of Ken's stable ways, how he's always on time for everything and usually early. The way he kept his personal records and knowing how reliability he is with peoples' financial profiles."

Sara stood and stared out the window. "I can't tell you how proud I am that Ken ordered the ring from a mail catalog."

Sara sat back down in silence as she twisted her hand, watching the sparkles on each angle of the mount. It made the five-point diamond appear even larger. Her ring was entwined and mounted in a ten-carat, yellow-gold setting.

Karen felt obligated to voice an "ohh and ahh." For a brief moment, Karen felt relaxed.

Then Sara went on mentioning about receiving their matching bands to use later. She said, "Ken was a real flirt." Then Sara shivered as she looked at Karen. "I'm not cold."

Trying to reach past her own toiling and raw pain, Karen whined, "I remember those feelings, Sara." It felt as though Sara unintentionally was pouring salt into a wound. She was raw with grief.

Karen excused herself and placed a roast in the oven for it was almost dinner time and Jud would be coming home soon. Knots kept welling up until perspiration beaded.

But Sara went on like a fluttering bird going "Chirp, chrip, chirp." Sara mentioned the house Ken had passed by on his way to work and let her know it was a one-floor plan.

Sara, trying to imitate Ken, said, "It should be a great starter home for us. It had a living room, three bedrooms, one bath, a large eat-in kitchen, and we ought to take a look."

"What did you say?"

Sara smiled. "We set an appointment for a showing. I told him to call me afterward as I poked him in the shoulder, kidding with him. The pun brought a belly laugh to Ken, and it caused me to laugh also. He's so levelheaded and knowledgeable. I find that highly attractive."

"That's nice," Karen grunted, knowing Sara would miss the pain in her voice.

"I'm trying to do things for Ken like you do for Jud," Sara went on. "It's hard, but I'm learning. I want him to feel his self worth. I see it, I think, in the amber of his eyes. I only have you to thank for being such a role model to me. Karen, he's a dedicated man at work and with me. Ken and Jud are a lot alike when it comes to doing business and taking care of us women, don't you think?"

Karen could only nod her head while placing the pillow in her lap.

"Ken wanted to assured me that his hard work at the bank was in the best interest for him to advance. He told me he felt guilty for not spending more time with me than he had. Ken requested a change in his work schedule from Jud since it would cause Ken to be out of town for a few days." Sara, hunched up her shoulders in plea. "Sorry, Karen, Jud will be working longer hours at the bank for awhile."

Karen sank further into the sofa.

Sara rattled on nonstop. "Oh, I didn't tell you. We ate all the ten little square burgers with pickles and all five fries. We were stuffed and Ken moaned all the way home."

Karen held tight onto the pillow, rocking back and forth. "Who wouldn't be ballooned after all that food."

Karen nervously bit her bottom lip. While watching, she said, "We have a lot to be thankful for." Karen could hardly contain herself. It was hard to sit there and be silent. She wanted so badly to make Sara stop the nonsense. She opened her mouth, but realized Sara was in her own little world.

Karen moved into the kitchen and saw Sara making jesters and talking. What had she said? She found herself staring out the kitchen window, wondering if Jud would even come home tonight. She closed her eyes and started praying. *I know I don't seek You, out very often, but I'm in a hurting mess. Help!*

Sara stepped into the kitchen bringing in her glass and the tea pitcher. "Do you need any help with the pot roast or anything?"

Karen wheeled around pushing her fist at her sides. Thinking better than answering her right then, she grabbed a pot and began making stew tomatoes.

Sara sat on the bar stool. "Karen, Ken walked me home in pure silence. Matter of fact, neither one of us said a word. We walked unhurriedly hand in hand to Mom's front door. He took his free arm and placed it around my shoulder and drew me close to him. Ken pointed out that Mom had left the porch light on." She tapped her fingers annoyingly on the counter. "You know she would be waiting up inside and you know how old-fashioned my parents are."

"Sara, I do know. I've witnessed their actions before." Karen shook her head and muttered, "Glad it was you instead of me. They are a force to reckon with."

Sara gave a warm smile. "Ken's a head and a half taller than I am even with the three-inch heels. He surprised me. He leaned over and hurriedly kissed me before he left. Karen, I felt heat of real passion roll from him. I wasn't in any better shape. I had to rest against the doorway to gain strength while waving to him long after his car had driven away. I want a relationship just like yours and Jud. Isn't it grand we all are friends?"

In the kitchen, Karen bent over to tend to the pot roast. She turned the heat down to low and added the stewed tomatoes. In silence, she began making cherry dumplings while Sara swung around on the stool.

Sara stated, "Did you know Ken had already asked Dad for my hand in marriage before today?"

"No, I didn't. When did they talk?"

"About a month ago."

"What did your dad say to him?"

"Dad told him, 'You better take darn good care of her. I couldn't have had a more loving-devoted daughter than her.'"

Karen couldn't resist a smile as a vivid scene came to mind. Sara's dad was very protective.

"I think Ken was touched by his approval because of my father's declining health. He also noticed my mom standing behind Dad while she took out her hankie to wipe at her tears." Sara's smile slipped. "You know with Dad being in the wheelchair most of the time you can tell he has lost weight. His bones are beginning to show through his clothes."

Karen stretched and walked over to her friend, giving her a much needed hug. It seemed to help her too.

Sara reached around and returning the hug, tightening the embrace. Both women had tears, but Karen knew it was for different reasons.

Sara looked up at Karen and saw her pacing. She headed over to Sara and shooed her toward the living room door. Jumping down from the stool, Sara adjusted herself, grabbed her diary, and stopped in the doorway. Sara looked over her shoulder.

"While waiting on Ken to get back in town, I've taken another design assignment. I've procrastinated long enough. It's an entire office, but it can be finished before his return."

Sara put her arm around Karen again. "I'm glad we're the best of friends. Thanks again for the tea and your time. I'm sure your ears are tender. Mom will need my help shortly with Dad." Stepping down from the porch, she said, "I'll call you after I see the house. Tell Jud when he gets home that I said hi."

Sara tapped on her diary. She would pen everything down about the house as soon as Ken took her to see it. She knew Karen would want to hear everything.

Dear diary,

It's been a few days since I last wrote. Ken called this morning when he got back to check and see if the time he arranged for a viewing of the house was okay. He asked, "Does this meet with your schedule, Miss Sara?" Dear diary, Ken makes me laugh. He's such a gentleman and handsome too!

Pausing her writing, she checked her appointment book. The design job had just been finished and was checked. Sara rubbed her chin, thinking Ken's timing couldn't be any better. It worked out perfectly.

Poised with her pen again, she continued writing.

"Ken, hey, can you swing by and pick me up?"

"Be there on a dime."

Boy, he got there early. We went to see the house. As we pulled up, I was so impressed. We reached for each other's hand, and he gave me a little squeeze. I squeezed his back, wanting to make sure he felt very important and honored.

We stood for a moment and stared. We loved the whitewashed bungalow. It was surrounded by a white picket fence with ivy vines overlapping. I noticed it came with a one-car garage that Ken had forgotten to mention. I loved the location and everything about the house. It seemed to have great bones. It was not far from my parents' home. Plus, it was close to his work. It also was near the bus line, should there be a need. It was a win-win situation! I'm so happy.

Goodnight, diary. Mom's calling.

Sara

The next day became cloudy. The sky hovered with a mass of thick gray covering right before it rained. The family clothes were hanging outside to dry. Sara quickly ran to gather the slacks, shirts, and skirts. It was good they were mostly dried. All it took was very little ironing for the clothes to be completed.

Hello diary.

It's Thursday. I explained to Ken the way the house seemed to be designed just for us. I was so excited and wanted him to make the house purchase right away so all the rooms could be finished before our wedding day when we moved in. Dear diary, I asked him. Nothing more was mention by either one of us today about the purchase of the house. I went on as normal as could be. Just waiting.

Well, diary, I'm closing for now.

Sara

The days became too rushed. The days turned into weeks, but today was different. Sara look out as the sun came up and the clouds were like fluffy cotton balls. They danced acrossed the sky in all kinds of shapes. She wondered what her friend Karen was doing and dialed her number.

On the third ring, she answered.

"Hello?"

"Hi, Karen. How are you feeling?"

"Sara, it's good to hear from you. I've been working some long hours. Oh, my aching back."

"I've been missing you too. Would you like me to come over and rub your back? Or is that saved for Jud? Just kidding."

"Come on over and talk with me. Can you come now?"

"Be right there!" Sara waltzed across the street with her diary in hand and humming a song.

Karen had the screen door ajar and greeted her there. She took her diary, motioned Sara to come in, and began to read. As they sat in the parlor, Karen motioned where the pot of brewed tea sat and for Sara to help herself.

Karen looked up and said, "Where's the house? Did he get it?"

Sara smiled. "It took him forty-five days before he had the deed in his name. Karen, when he called me and suggested that I meet him at the house, which is located on Grove Street, I squealed. Upon arriving to the house, he gave me a lasting kiss, and he had unsteady breathing. Ken handed over the key to our cottage home. Karen, I felt like a queen and was mentally in awe of what a great match we made. I told him that he was my man. Karen, getting the paint for each room was exciting and unnerving, but I'm ready to design. Can you help?"

"Yes. Let's do it."

# 3

Sara and Karen began in the master bedroom. They used a sea-foam color in the blue-green shade. They did the trimming in warm shades of sand.

Sara stopped Karen before they entered the spare bedroom. "I want to achieve a country look. Quit turning up your nose and help."

Karen gave a titter as she picked up the brush. She mentioned to Sara that she felt needed, and a huge smile appeared across her face. Stepping down from the ladder and glancing around the room, she looked into the mirror by Sara. It reflected the morning clouds hanging in the sky. They moved into the kitchen where a sunny yellow color had been selected, and it was very bright. Sara and Karen worked long into the night, hanging cafe curtains of white-and-red checks. Karen was amused that Sara had made them from feed sacks. Karen stroked a figurine of a mother hen with baby chicks and reached for the rooster sculpture and placed them on top of the plant divider. It separated the kitchen from the living room. It took Karen and Sara one month before the rooms were completed.

Now the wedding would occur. Karen knew Ken would not see the rooms or their beauty until Sara's and his honeymoon. Looking back, Karen saw it had been a great journey for Sara and Ken. Time had passed to quickly. A new chapter of togetherness had begun. It was a new launch. Karen considered Sara and Ken had the foundation as "One" with the journey, of the march of life, commenced. She heard their "I dos," and it followed in the days of their new home.

Karen, veering off, thought how Ken had announced to Sara after they were married and for all to hear, "I have been patiently waiting for you and our honeymoon." Then he bent and picked her up and stated, "Darling, this will last us forever!"

Karen could see that they were more in love with each other than ever. Karen had stood by her friend Sara as she stated, "Work is blissful, but coming home to Ken will be such a joy." Karen felt her words sting her heart. It was difficult for Karen to watch the way Ken flirted with Sara. But seeing Sara's eyes only reflected a promise of endearment. It was love forever.

Karen reflected on the fact that only a short time of exactly nine months to the day of Sara's marriage, Timmy was born. Wow, what a shocking experience and an exciting day it proved to be for Sara. Karen recalled how they had been in touch with each other during the last month of Sara's pregnancy. She had been to the hospital three different times already with false labor. Ken had the routine down to the last minute. He came home most days early from work just to be with her. Sara was amused about him being a nervous wreck. After all, this would be his first time being a dad.

Karen recalled that day vividly.

Sara had called and said, "Oh, Karen, thank goodness I reached you. It's time for the baby to be born. I was wondering if you would come over and mind the house and phone for me?"

"Sure. Jud is out of town, so I'll be right there." Stepping outside, Karen had checked the front door to make sure it was locked. She could tell it was going to be a hot day as she watched steam rise off the pavement. The forecast called for a high of ninety.

"Hello." Karen pecked on the screen door.

Sara waddled to the door. "Thank goodness you're here. I don't think Ken believes me when I say it is really time for me to go to the hospital. He's in the backyard mowing. Can you get him for me?"

Karen opened their back door, waving her arms wildly to flag him. She yelled then screamed, "This time it's for real. You need to take Sara to the hospital. Now!"

Ken tossed her a confused expression that quickly turned to concern. "Coming." He im-mediately turned off the mower and rushed inside the house.

Sara mentioned that Ken was a clean freak. He had gone to their room, showered, and soon reappeared with wet hair and fresh clothes.

Sara, being a little impatient, said, "Ken, what part of now didn't you understand?" She seemed to know the timing was right to head for the hospital.

She had told Karen earlier about the back pains. Her back had twinges and aches most of the day, but it was the twitch in the side that really got Sara's attention. It just would not go away no matter what she did or tried.

Again, not so pleasantly, she called out to Ken, "Let's go.'"

Karen gave a forlorn smile as she ushered Sara and Ken out the door. She followed closely behind to help encourage them.

Patting Sara on the shoulder, never in a hurry, Ken grabbed the packed bag and gently helped Sara into the front seat of the car. He made sure the windows were down as the heat seemed to bear down on the car.

As he began backing up, she gripped his hand, causing him to flinch as she yelled a most terrible scream. "Eek eek," and she began puffing.

Turning his head in her direction, he asked, "What kind of scream was that? I've never heard such a noise! It sounded like it was right in my ear."

Karen came out waving her arms. "What's wrong?"

Ken slammed on the brakes, parked the car, and jumped out. He left Karen standing and Sara still in the car.

Karen looked at Sara in puzzlement but ran into the house after Ken. He was on the phone with the hospital. She heard Ken explained that his wife was in labor. He stuttered out their address before hanging up the phone. Ken returned to the car. Karen held the front door open as Ken began slowly and carefully helping to move Sara back into the house. Sara again had another pain. This time, it bent her over, and she pushed.

Karen fanned Sara. "Help is on the way."

The ambulance EMTs arrived at the exact same moment. They took control, barking out orders to Ken and Karen. "Get the towels."

Obediently, Ken got the supplies, and Karen hurried to Sara's side.

Sara let out another howl until her mouth moved without sound. The EMT had the stretcher brought in from the ambulance.

She quietly sent up a prayer: *Be with my friend Sara.*

The EMT placed Sara on the sofa. They propped her feet up. As they were taking her pulse, Sara screamed to the top of her lungs. "The baby's coming." Then Sara passed out. Karen just stared.

What seemed like a long time was only seconds before Sara regained consciousness. The pain weld deeper, and her water broke. An EMT placed a cool cloth on Sara's forehead. Karen and Ken took turns trying to assure Sara everything was all right. Sara began pushing once again, and on the third push, the baby's head crowned.

Karen, Ken, and the EMTs soon knew the baby was present.

"It's a boy," they shouted, and the baby cried. Karen was beside herself.

Upon the examination, which checked to see if Sara and the baby were all right, the ambulance personnel looked at Ken and Karen. "I see we are no longer needed." They extended their congratulations to the couple and nodded to Karen as they turned and left.

Ken beamed from ear to ear. "Sara, let's name our boy 'Timmy.' It was my grandfather's name."

She humbly nodded. "Sounds great."

Now, that was how Timmy was born and named then and there, and it began. Still another march of life.

Karen felt so sick. She couldn't remember a time when she had felt so bad. She thought a new flu bug may have gotten to her. She felt weak and tired. She just couldn't shake it. The flu had made its rounds at the beauty bar shop where she worked. Most of her coworkers had taken their turn being off work due to the virus. Karen decided to go to the doctor, thinking perhaps an antibiotic was needed, but the visit had changed her flu thoughts. "Karen, you are pregnant."

The news caused her to go into shock. Doctor March kept his hand on her and called for the nurse to find three ounces of pure unsweetened orange juice that he wanted Karen to drink.

Weakly, Karen remarked, "I don't even like orange juice!"

The nurse firmly held Karen's head up with one hand. "Drink up. It will help you."

After seeing there was no way out, she drank the juice and lay back down to rest. Fear entered Karen when the nurse suggested calling Jud. She willed herself to calm down. Soon she felt a little stronger, but the shocking word still rang in her head. "Pregnant!"

Dr. March had placed Karen into the recovery room to make sure she was all right. He told her to rest and that he would be back later to look in on her.

Karen lay there and reflected on how she first met Jud. There was a weekly reading group being held at the local library. She and her best friend Sara had attended it. Both came by bus. When they arrived for the evening service and walked into the room, both ladies were surprised to find the chairs placed in a

SUSAN KAY BOX BRUNNER

circular position. They took their seats over to the left to be closer to the speaker's table. Also, they wanted out of the draft that was whipping up their skirts through the open door.

Sara poked Karen. "Turn your head to the right."

Karen did as instructed, and there walking in was the dreamiest guy she had ever seen. It was as if he was in slow motion. She could barely talk. In a childlike voice, she uttered, "Thank you, Sara."

She found herself scanning him over from head to toe. As she glanced around the room she saw other female eyes following him also. How handsome and demure he looked. Those broad shoulders and tapered waist made a statement in itself as well as the way he carried his attractive stature. So awesome was the way his arm muscles flexed in a suit. He came across so natural and confident, yes, and even rich. The mere look of him made Karen go weak in the knees. Sara was tapping Karen's shoulder, trying to get her attention. As Karen turned toward Sara the mystery man smiled and her gaze was pinned to him. Karen was lost in his deep emerald-green eyes. She felt the atmosphere tingle, drawing her to him. She would have drowned had it not been for Sara. Karen realized the need to escape from him.

Sara leaned into Karen. "Hello. Hello." Karen's breath was shallow. She willed herself to get up. She made herself walk on shaky legs toward him while saying to Sara, "Wow."

"Take it easy, Karen!"

Both girls at Karen's request stayed close to each another. They offered help to the teacher. Karen appeared busy, really busy. She gave quick glances at the new guy, but at one point, to her surprise standing next to him was another new person. Both seemed to know each other.

Karen jarred Sara. "There, Sara, over by the pole," Karen whispered, nodding toward the guys. "Who is he?"

Sara seemed to be curious as well. Sara, being the smart one, went to the teacher and inquired. "Have the new fellows been introduced?"

Mr. Nite, the professor, instructed Sara to rush over there and get their names and make both men feel welcome. He motioned for her to go ahead and take Karen. "Remember," he said. "Introduce yourselves."

Both Sara and Karen took their time and did not rush, but as composed as one could be, they went to the area where the guys were standing and brought them cookies and punch. A lot of people had already gathered around them from the reading group, which were mostly women.

Karen appealed to Sara, "I will not do this." Sara rolled her eyes and took Karen by the arm.

She balanced the cookies, and announced, "We are meeting them and we are doing it now!"

Karen tried to question when she caught the sight of the first man walking over toward them. The man extended his hand. "Hi, my name is Jud, and this is my friend Ken. We saw the posting of the reading study group to be here at the library.

Karen accepted his warm hand but immediately withdrew it. She crossed her arms, feeling reluctant to chat. She opened her mouth to speak, but her tongue wouldn't work. It felt like cotton was in it. Not a word came out.

Jud spoke again. "I see you must be a regular here, and your name tag reads Karen." He gave her a mischievous smile. "Is that you?" His eyebrows went up. "Is one of the drinks for me?"

Karen glanced Sara's way for help but found she was busy in conversation with Ken. *Think, Karen*, she told herself. Taking her own advice, she willed herself to clear her throat and reached a hand forward to the gentleman, giving him a glass of punch. "Of course, my name is Karen. I didn't know there were any flyers posted on the town's welcome board, but I am glad you both ran across them and came."

She knew Jud could see though her tough act. She considered the way he smiled when he took her hand again and said, "Karen, would you like to go out sometime with me? Maybe have dinner and a movie?"

Pulling her hand away from him this time took everything within her.

Her voice seemed a little too high-pitched, even for her, as she answered, "Sure." Karen turned to walk where Sara stood, but Sara had the same idea and they bumped into each other. Both Karen and Sara stared at each other for a moment, and then they got the giggles.

Professor Nite gathered the crowd for their weekly session, and the time flew by. He was always a brilliant speaker. They were at the end of their question-and-answer segment.

The girls spoke in unison while looking at the new men, "See you next week if you can make it."

The girls waved. "Good night to everyone."

Still nervously laughing, Karen and Sara left the meeting place to catch their bus home.

A few days later, Karen heard the phone ring. She had been dusting and put the cloth down. On the third ring. she answered. "It's about time you called." She thought it was Sara, but instead the voice had a crisp, very deep tenor sound. It was Jud.

Her free hand flew to her face in embarrassment. Holding the phone down, she muttered under her breath, "Oh my, oh my." Trying to compose herself she placed the line to her ear. She went to speak, but Jud was talking.

Karen had not heard a word he said, until he asked, "Well, is it okay?"

Hesitating for only a moment, she wondered what to say. What if she answered yes and she should have said no? She heard the amusement in his voice. She, for some unexplained reason, trusted she was giving the right answer to him when she said, "Okay."

"Great, I'll pick you up at your house this Friday at six."

She hadn't even said another word for she had hung up the phone. Friday was only two days away and yet it seemed like a long time.

Karen had called Sara to let her know about the mysterious call from Jud, but she was on a design assignment.

Friday evening came, and Karen was peeking out her window when she saw him drive up. Jud had on a cream-colored shirt with khaki slacks and was wearing leather brown sandals. His crooked smile showed a dimple and it only added to his attraction. Her parents were on the porch and made small talk with Jud. She quickly placed her sweater around her shoulders and covered their bareness. She had worn her baby blue linen dress. She fastened the buckle on her flat T-strap shoes before heading outside.

Jud greeted her with such confidence. She felt so giddy. They walked to his car and he seated her in the Barracuda. He was still smiling as he got in on the other side. The radio was low and playing a song by Frank Sinatra. She had hoped they were not going anywhere to fancy.

They stopped in front of the movie house. Karen took a deep breath as he came around to let her out and another deep breath as he ushered her inside.

He stopped at the concession stand and bought a barrel container of buttered popcorn and two extra large cherry colas. The old theater with the velvet drapes of red still had their classic feel. The lights were low, and the usher holding a flashlight, looked at their tickets, and then showed them to their seats. As they went to sit down, Jud's fragrance wafted under her nose. Her eyes needed to adjust for the lack of light. Karen reached for some popcorn and noticed he was watching her. It made her feel cautious but happy. The feature, *Gone with the Wind*, was her favorite. She hadn't seen the movie since she was ten years old and her mother had taken her.

The lights went down and both were brought into the movie with the greatest intent. Time went too quickly. The lights went up and intermission came. Karen called her parents to let them know where they were. Jud strolled over to her and again they took their seats to enjoy the second half. Jud slipped his arm around her shoulder during the second half. It felt natural, Karen thought. At the end of the movie people were cheering for Rhett or crying for Scarlet. Karen felt mixed emotions and none were about the movie. Jud took her straight home, walked her to the door, and tried to reinact Rhett's leaving, but he busted into laughter. Karen was amazed, amused, and befuddled all at the same time.

He nodded as he gave her a hand shake. "I'll be in touch."

She couldn't get over his dazzling eyes.

He turned and walked down the steps of her house. He had left her standing in awe. As Karen thought back, he had interested her. She only wanted to know him more.

They continued to date. They found it easy to converse with each other. He shared from their very beginning that he felt they had a real future together. She felt flattered. She knew he put a lot of thought into what they talked about for he had asked her to look deep and be honest with him. He told her he wanted to do the same if there were to be any hopes of a potential togetherness.

One evening while sitting on the front porch, she heard him pray. "I need a little help." His face was looking upward. "Hello, are you listening?"

# 4

---

Jud was a business-minded person, and he looked and talked his part 24-7. He mostly wore a two-piece Lord Frederick business suit. The combo of black, navy blue, or gray was striking. His contrast-ing tie and matching socks set him apart from all other men. When he spoke, it was with authority and people stopped to listen.

On this sunny day, it began like any other. The sky was bright, and there was hardly a cloud to be seen. There was a soft western breeze fanning in the air.

Jud called Karen's work place. "Hello, Karen. I need to see you today!"

She felt his urgency when he pressed to see her.

"I'll pick you up within the next three hours."

Karen answered, "All right, but I can't talk right now. I'm at the shampoo bowl rinsing out a client.

He heard her high spirits come across the line. In the background, he had heard water. He knew she would have soapsuds splashed all around. Jud had observed Karen enough to know she would waltz through her clients. She wouldn't take any breaks, and perhaps she would reschedule her last two people.

He parked in front of the salon. Her coworkers were so vain. They flirted with him unmercifully as he stepped inside. Karen threw up her hand and quickly rushed to his side and all but ushered him out. Jud was amused.

He paused after opening the door so she could slide into the car. He had the windows down so they could enjoy the breeze. He stopped the car and she looked the river. Its flow and ripples had a relaxing sound to it. Jud popped open the trunk and pulled out a blanket and a picnic basket.

Karen helped spread the blanket and unloaded the basket. She offered Jud a bite. He acted like a bird opening his mouth.

They laughed and teased each other unmercifully. While holding her hand, a serious look came into his eyes. "Karen, what I need to say to you is not intended for you to get hurt, but I feel you have the right to know. It's about my past."

Karen gave Jud her full attention. She sat up straight, starring at him in question.

She knew he was talking to her straight from the hip. He left no doubt in her imagination on what he said. It was earth-shattering. Karen not wanting to sit in judgment wondered if she ever really knew him. She realized at that moment she would begin keep-ing little secret thoughts collected and concealed about her true feelings toward him.

Karen felt the need to talk with her friend. She knew Sara would never understand that Jud had a pervious experience with the opposite sex. How could she explain he had been with another woman? Or maybe there was more? Karen sat there and thought what was she to do? She was both lacking in experience and she didn't have any knowledge on the subject. She began thinking how inadequate she was for Jud. She faced the fact; she certainly was not woman enough for him. Knowing she was not qualified on intimate ways she kept mute from talking about it to anyone. Her emotions became uncontrollable. Her temper flared and she became short with her clients. She avoided Sara. Frustration surrounded her most of the time. She felt she could trust no one. It left her with many questions, and without somebody to confide in. Karen spent time wondering if she should seek out her mom and ask her questions, but decided to dismissed the idea for it would be way too embarrassing. She spoke to the air. "I can't give his secret up. If Sara knew, what would she think about Jud? How could I ever ask her about the birds and the bees?"

No, no, she wouldn't discuss these issues either. Karen felt uncomfortable in her feelings and she really did not understand why. She was experiencing a problematic search of her inner self and she held no peace or answers.

Jud had phoned Karen twelve times since they last spoke. She had stalled him most of the time. She still needed time to sort out her feelings concerning his revelation.

Looking out the window, Karen saw the grayish clouds covering the sky. They threatened rain. The first drop appeared and so did a very polished-looking Jud. Her stomach went into knots. She was excited to see him but puzzled. She opened the door and invited him into the parlor. He placed himself at one end of the sofa and stared at her. She let herself sit in a straight-back chair.

Her mother peered around the corner and gave Jud a smile. Jud stood. They exchanged a friendly greeting before Kate nodded and turned back into the kitchen.

Jud sat facing Karen. He had his hands folded and laying on his lap. "Karen, you keep turning me away, avoiding me. I can't stand it. My request to see you on this occasion might be hard, but it is a must. I have to tell you things. It is so necessary. That's why I'm here." Twisting his hands, she saw his forehead was beaded with perspiration.

"Karen, there is just no easy way for me to tell you! It's about a teen named Eurlene." Hesitating, he stood and began pacing the floor, then stopped. He sat on the rug in front of her. He had pleading eyes and outstretched hands. "I made the teen acquaintance the last six weeks of my senior year in high school. She was a transfer student from another state. Eurlene was placed in most of my classes. Our homeroom teacher Mr. Keith, paired both of us together. He told me I was an honor student and had extra duties to help other students achieve. He said Eurlene needed my help to catch up her studies. It was for extra credit and added toward my grade for graduation."

Jud shook his head and diplomatically said, "That's when things happened, Karen. I lost my self-control. I want you to completely understand my situation." Raking his hand through his hair, he spoke. "Eurlene was an exceptional woman. She was easy to the eye and very leggy. She was extremely mature in places that matter most to guys. Her conduct was unquestionably way too forward. I had a simple crush on her, and she came on to me."

Karen sat stock still as he went on.

"She excelled in her classes and made learning appealing. My feelings for her grew until I thought we were both in love. Eurlene was a real flirt, not only to me but to everyone. She became a challenge to all of us guys as if she were an Oscar or trophy to acquire."

Jud rolled up his sleeves. "I should have been strong and sought God for guidance, but..."

Karen being stirred moved closer and extended her hand to Jud as they sat on the floor.

He seemed to relax slightly under her touch. "On the evening of the graduation, we were to attend the senior class party. My dad loaned me the car to pick up Eurlene. When I arrived, she was not there. The house sat empty."

He related how a neighbor came out and said, "'If you're looking for them, they're gone. The man and girl moved out last night in the wee hours. They didn't leave a forwarding address either. Sorry.'

Jud told how he had ambled up the steps and found a hand-written note address to him. It was lying on the ground. It must have fallen from its place between the doors. "Karen, I went numb. I put my hands to my face and there wasn't any feeling in them. My tears dropped but I could only see their wetness. All my strength was zapped from me. I found myself at the nearby park. Sitting next to a lamp pole I opened the note and it read: 'Dear Jud, I need to inform you I was pregnant with your child.'"

Karen was all but sitting on his lap. She scooted closer and tried not to interrupt him. She only wanted to offer him support and comfort.

Abruptly, Jud stood and raised a hand to stop her. He began pacing the floor and poked his right hand into his pants pocket. "Eurlene wrote that she had an abortion. Being with child was not for her nor staying pregnant. It was not an option. She said it would have ruined her life and her career."

Jud stared at Karen intensely, but went on. "Eurlene said she had never wanted to settle down. She viewed marriage as a handicap, and she never wanted to have children."

Karen went colorless and gasped. "Oh." She quickly tried to hide her surprise and hurt. She hadn't realized she had spoken with such hopelessness out loud. *Jud doesn't really want to marry me. He had wanted to marry Eurlene.*

Jud was broken by Karen's reaction, but he continued in a low whisper. "Karen, my lungs felt injured. It was as if they were punctured. All the air within me vanished. I could no longer breathe." He beat his hands on the ground. "It's not fair. I felt used, hurt, rejected, and yes, even dirty. Karen, she had one purpose in mind when she left town. It was never to see me again. I tried to find just a trace of her, but it was to no avail. Karen, time marches on for all of us. I hadn't thought about her in years. I had moved on with my life successfully. Then I was blessed when I met sweet wonderful you."

He had suffered for being so private about his life and he finally had made himself vulnerable when he shared the past with Karen. He let himself be hopeful to embark on a fresh new level of his association with her. Suddenly he felt refreshed. He had a new rawness as he spoke with Karen. "I pledge that day to become the most successful business entrepreneur I could be or my name was not Judwin Day."

Karen ached from thinking about how Jud had turned her away when she reached out to him. She didn't even get an opportunity to try and ease his pain. She was disappointed first and then she became very furious. Karen was hurt. Words and actions had sent bitter messages to her mind and pierced her heart. She took up the felt burden by doing more at work. A few days later after mulling and giving consideration to all the information Jud had alleged she came to the conclusion. She would fight for Jud. Secretly and prayfully. *I've fallen so much for him and I'm in too deep.*

Karen was determined she could make him take an interest in her. Yes. She was going to battle him with her intellect. After all she was smart. Wasn't she?

Karen and Sara met with Jud and Ken the following Wednesday evening at the reading group. Karen had avoided Jud so she could reclaim her thoughts about him, but as their eyes met, she knew they held quite an attraction for each other. Something was in the air, and she was not in control.

Karen felt drawn as he huskily announced, "Ken and I are going for a cherry Coke and a sandwich. Karen, Sara, would you like to come?"

Karen nodded while Sara pulled her into the car. Things progressed from that evening forth for her and Jud. She decided not to mention his past again. She concentrated in making their friendship blossom.

Jud liked life to be scheduled as much as possible so Karen arranged for them to bowl on Thursdays, ball games on Fridays, and she scheduled skating on Saturdays. Together they attended church services on Sundays, and she looked forward to their promised long walks that came afterward. Karen saw him daily as if on automatic pilot for six months. After skating one Saturday evening, she was given a suggestion from Jud on how they should get married. Nothing to her seemed romantic, but he had offered. Karen was excited anyhow and ready to say yes. She wondered how she would present to Jud that she intended to keep working. She hoped he would be in agreement.

Karen viewed Jud as a solid man and when he used his logic on the reasons why they should marry such as what they had in common, how practical they were together, and what a terrific couple they made. Just one thing was missing. He hadn't told her that he loved her. Karen knew everything he said was true. But with happiness and a heavy heart, she would agree. She thought they were made for each other. But she held her tongue and never uttered her deep desire to hear his words of love. Time marched on and Karen felt like the walls were caving in. The air would not flow fast enough for her lungs to inhale. She felt relief when she got wind that Jud was officially going to ask for her hand in marriage. He had spoken with her father about marriage and Donald had agreed.

Jud made arrangements at a certain restaurant to surprise Karen.

The phone rang as Karen was about to step into the soak tub. Grabbing her robe, she rushed to the phone. "Hello?"

Jud was on the other end. "Karen, I want us to go out tonight. Let's change our routine?"

She felt special. "What time? I'll be ready." The phone line cracked, or was it his voice, when he croaked, "Six."

Karen looked at the clock, threw back on her clothes and asked her mom to go shopping. She purchased an evening gown. Looking into the mirror she was pleased with its effects. The dress was sheer and free flowing. The front had a boat neck line and the back plunged to the waist. Karen glowed and beamed all over. When evening came, her dad and mother greeted Jud at the door and then called for Karen's entrance.

All three pair of eyes turned and were on her. She noticed Jud's had a trace of wickedness in his. He reached out his hand for hers as he glided her to the car. He leaned on the door and dropped her a kiss. Karen's stomach began fluttering.

The restaurant was awesome. Classical music set the mood as it played softly in the background. A smooth voice gently announced, "'Thinking of You' is now being played by Harry Ruby."

Karen turned to face Jud at their table, but he had dropped to one knee and was looking up at her as if he was ready to propose.

She noticed his lopsided grin and winked, as he reached for her hand again.

She was experiencing butterflies in her stomach as he asked, "Karen will you marry me?"

Karen shyly answered, "Yes."

The announcer got everyone attention. He let the audience know about Jud's proposal. All eyes were fixed on them. She could hardly breathe for the endearment had wrapped her heart. The people responded with a cheery "Hip, hip, hurray!"

Karen felt the heat rise to her face while Jud stole a kiss.

Karen knew she loved him. She also wanted to be everything and more to him. She wanted all the benefits and extras that marriage would bring. She was determined not to settle for just winning his highest respect for her.

A great wedding took place in an old Victorian church. It was assumed to be built in the early 1800s. The quaint church sat in a more established part of town in Ohio where mature trees make an archway all along the streets. Inside the church to the right of the front sat a rather old pipe organ with aged gold pipes extending to the ceiling. The aisle ways were narrow and sloped very steeply leading to the front of the auditorium. Vanilla-scented candles were lit and the building inside glowed with enchantment.

Coming down the aisle it appeared to Karen as if she were floating on air wearing a fitted Chantilly full-length wedding dress with a tail trailing three pews behind. As she walked, gliding down the aisle alongside her father, linked arm in arm, memories passed from one to the other through their eye contact. Donald flashed a broad smile to give much needed reassurance for the moment at hand.

Karen looked toward the front and saw Jud with his best man Ken, and he looked very demure. Jud was in a gray, long-tail tuxedo with a white rose boutonniere, and he stood faithfully at the front of the church, waiting and noticeably having eyes only for her.

Now, the flowers brought a new level of warmth and elegance to the room. The divine scent mingled and floated throughout the entire building.

Over five hundred people attended, and the church was packed. There were no seats left so some guests had to stand. Looking around there were people lined up outside the church door just trying to get a glance. Heads were bobbing up and down, but the ushers had to stand firm; they kept the doors open yet guarded, allowing no one in.

The lady attendant had taken care of everything, making sure all the details did not become issues. It went very smoothly and reverently, as if one had stepped back in time once again.

The time came to pronounce them husband and wife. Karen was waiting and anticipating the announcement, being pronounced his wife, Mrs. Karen Day, for she would no longer be Karen Page. Her stomach was in a rage and her heart was pounding so hard she thought all could hear. Oh! The announcement was made. Karen looked at Jud and his lopsided grin, showing the deep dimples which melted her heart. She saw in his eyes the passion he wanted to share. Karen silently said, "He's mine."

Then he gave her a kiss, and they seemed to melt as one. What a kiss! The heat flamed, and sensation traveled down Jud and through Karen. She was sure both felt the electricity. Jud was trying to steady her as they walked forward toward the reception hall. However, she could feel his strength on her arm and knew he was holding on to her to get a better balance of himself. Then all the people cheered.

The reception immediately followed the wedding ceremony. The photographer and guests' cameras just kept flashing. Arranged at the special table were two flat cakes, one chocolate and the other strawberry. The eye-catching wedding cake, smack dab in the middle of the specially designed table, was five tiers high. There was a tiny plastic ladder placed on each side of the profile cake from the top going to the bottom. It had a porcelain-looking groom on one ladder and a porcelain-looking bride on the other. A lit miniature pond was at the bottom, surrounding the cake with floating-fresh flowers which were placed perfectly all around. The wedding cake was the envy of every woman there, but it was not the only thing, so was she.

After the reception was over, the rice was thrown, Karen's bouquet was heisted up in the air, and the doves were let loose. Jud and Karen left to go on their honeymoon. Karen was caught up in the moment. She felt like a queen. Her day had been perfect and now she took the risk and kissed her king.

Reality set in. The honeymoon clearly was not very well planned by Jud. He certainly had not discussed it with Karen, either. She had left their plans up to him. Their money budget just did not stretch as far as would be needed. If Karen had not found a wedding card with a hundred-dollar bill placed in her purse by a distant but favorite aunt, they would have slept in his car the first night. Karen, not knowing what to say, said the first thing that popped into her head. "Jud, don't you think Auntie is such a wonderful person? We must send her a special thank-you card."

Jud appeared stunned. "Yes, she was quite a lifesaver, and we should definitely thank her. Karen, we need to start looking for a place by the side of the road for us to pull over for the night." He paused. "Hey, I think I spotted something."

Sure enough there was a little single cottage near the edge of the road. A sign with bright yellow lights flashing off and on indicated "Vacant for the night." It appeared from nowhere.

Jud carefully carried Karen over the small threshold saying, "I want us to begin our journey right."

Karen blushed while nuzzling his neck. Although she kept her arms tightly around his shoulders a light whisper brushed his ear. "Me too."

Reluctantly, he placed her feet on the ground giving her a quick peck on the cheek. He spun around to retrieve their luggage from the car. As Karen stood there waiting, thoughts about her lack of experience—and this being her first time encountering this avenue with any man—and now it was to be with her true love, Jud. Chills began going up and down her spine from seeking all new expectations. No one had talked with her about what to do, or even how to anticipate an evening being alone with Jud. All those unexpressed feelings were pent up inside. She did not know how to vent them or even wondered if they would go away later.

# 5

When Jud walked though the door, Karen noticed he was holding only his luggage. He had set it down and made no attempt to retrieve hers. She saw no other baggage had been brought in for the night. Squirming, she began to panic, realizing her suitcase had been left at the church! She pleaded, "Jud we have to go back for my clothes and my makeup kit. They were left behind." Karen handled this the only way she knew how. She began to cry, which soon turned into a deep sob.

Jud seemed to think it was no big deal. "I'll share my T-shirt with you for the night. Or we both can be in our birthday suits, huh?"

Walking over to her he gave a little smile with one raised eyebrow and touched her chin. Karen frowned and pushed him away.

Jud sighed. "Karen, we do not have enough time or gasoline to go back and look for your luggage. You know the people from the reception hall would be long gone from the church by now. Your parents probably got the left-behind luggage and took it home with them or dropped it off at our place as with all our wedding gifts." Reaching for her he took her in his arms while soothingly speaking and stroking her long locks. "I am so sorry." Bending, he offered a kiss, but she froze on the spot in fear and forced the movement in her legs to bolt away from him.

"Karen, you are being so difficult. Why? Try to understand."
Jud paused. "I would stop at a store, but it's Sunday and you know
the 'blue law' is in effect. There are only churches and a few scat-
tered drugstores open during this time. Those stores are only for
emergency activities or uses. It will be all right. Trust me."

The slightly amused look on his face made Karen pouted all
the more. She moved toward the only door in their room and
closed it with a slam. Once outside a plan would work out in
her mind.

She slumped against the wall. "Yes, I will be a little more conservative with the makeup. What is still left on my face could be
blended and would work." She willed herself not to cry anymore,
for the makeup repair was a must.

She knew Jud must not see her without a made-up face. Also,
there would not be any more makeup gotten. Karen wanted only
to look beautiful for him. And in her mind, this was achieved
only if the makeup was on. Feeling more strength flowing back,
she stepped inside the cottage.

Jud looked more perplexed than ever. "We both are really tired
from today and truthfully, very drained. With the wedding, the
reception, and the picture taking, it's made for a long day! Not to
say, it was quite a drive here!" Then he slapped her teasingly on
the rump saying, "Hey Karen, I going to grab a shower. Want to
join me?"

Karen turned beet red and shook her head so he went on
ahead. After he finished toweling off, he popped into the doorway, motioning as an encouragement to Karen. "Come, hop in
and take the plunge. I am out," he teased.

Karen could not keep her eyes off where the towel did not
cover. His waist was so bronze and tapered, the hair leading from
the belly button. "Whoa girl," she said to herself. "Stop it! Get a
hold of yourself." But then she realized they had never been left
alone like this, at least not in any compromising way. Seeing him
half-naked and more left her whole body and mind woozy.

Jud was in a kidding mood, but Karen, being apprehensive, tried to avoid him at all cost. Suddenly it was an overpowering fear when she realized she did not know anything in the love-making department except for a little flirting and frolicking. She gave a quick look upward. *Help me.*

Speechless, she grabbed one of Jud's large T-shirts to use for a nightgown. Looking into the mirror, she saw how it swallowed her up. The neck came just above the chest, with the short sleeves looking like three-quarter lengths, and it was very baggy. The length hit below her knees. She wanted to shed tears for this was her special night. She had dream of this most of her life, but she was devoid of the white frilly chiffon peignoir. Seemed like a bad omen!

Karen moped thinking back to the night she came home and showed her mother the ring right after Jud had asked her to marry him. Her dad, Donald, stepped into the kitchen to check it out. He gave Karen a hug as he teased her. "You did all right catching him." He laughed as he walked out from the room.

Kate followed Karen to her bedroom and had a very private talk informing Karen about wearing a lovely free-flowing apparel for the first night as a bride.

Karen replied, "Can you go shopping with me?" Her mother patted her arm. "Let's go tomorrow?"

They got up early and shopped way until noon. Her mother finally saw the rack of exquisite gown sets and pointed with her index finger, showing Karen. Her mother had even helped her pick out this beautiful nightwear. They ended up spending an entire day together shopping. They purchased many things, but they especially shopped for the honeymoon night.

Karen was glad her mother gave some womanly advice and informed her that the nightwear was one of the signs to show him her purity. Kate told her, "No words are needed when Jud sees you, for he will understand the unspoken issue on your wedding night. Karen, just follow his lead."

Well, what was she to do now? It was too late to call her mother. How was this to be done? Boy, he wouldn't know the clues. Being in his T-shirt, she was flustered on the inside. Karen thought for a moment and did the only thing she could. She turned away from him in bed by rolling over. She laid on the other side on the bed's edge.

Jud scooted closer to Karen by saying sweet nothings in her ear, while mingling his hands in her sweet-smelling blonde hair. Karen moved closer to her edge of the bed. She felt Jud stiffen and knew he sensed something was wrong.

Karen, still being in grief about the nightwear and with panic setting in, placed a pillow between them for separation.

"Karen, sweetie, what is wrong?"

She could not answer him. She clung to the pillow. Karen could still feel his warmth and hardness even through the pillow.

Jud reached for her again.

Karen looked into his eyes. "Not tonight. Please." She was hoping to avoid any contact with him until she arrived home. She would be able to prepare and wear the special nightwear, so he would know and understand what she represented. She did not want to be embarrassed for the lack of knowledge she would need for their "Night's Event."

Jud arched his brow. She knew he was puzzled. Silently Jud slipped to a chair. Karen heard Jud pray, "Show me the way."

Once again, Jud opened his mouth to speak but shook his head instead. It was in the wee hours of the night and both only stare at each other. Karen felt like a deer caught in the headlights of an on-coming car. They didn't sleep. Carefully Jud removed the pillow between them and slowly crept over. He whispered, "Let's take our time getting personally acquainted with each other. We can build on our relationship before we take it to the next level."

Karen was shaking as she nodded okay. She felt a bitter rejection settle in. She had felt his need as he had moved closer toward her in bed. She had melted, and was waiting for the unexpected and unknown to happen. But to have an encounter with his speech instead of actions caused her to have relief and dissatisfaction. As she thought about this, she knew he would be understanding and have self-control for he had previously proven as much. As reality set in, Karen knew she was not really ready, and was glad for an agreement to halt things on this matter. As he turned over, lying on his right side, with one arm under his head and the other crumpling the sheet, he mumbled between his teeth, "Darn suitcases anyhow."

Karen heard him mumble something about giving him strength.

Long afterward Karen fell into a deep sleep. She felt his closeness and knew the pillow was gone but she feel deeper into slumber. Karen knew she should have felt relief at being cuddled in his arms early in the morning, but a roller coaster heading for a crash was more like it. Her emotions were unreal, and the saddest part was, she did not know precisely why. She became unsure of what to say or even how to act with him. There was a definite hidden strain there.

Jud continued approaching her, using compliments such as "You are lovely" and "I like how suitable we are," but Karen remained cold and aloof.

On occasion, she would reach up to touch his arm or face but never say anything. She couldn't help but see the physical effect it had on him, and at times it left him swollen. He would reach out in return, pulling her close, but she would say, "Not now Jud," then quickly position the table or place a chair between them.

At times when Jud would come up behind her while she was cleaning vegetables, it was to give her kisses on the neck; she could more than feel his presence before his entering the room as surely as if the wind had blown through the door.

Sometimes she would turn toward him with a heated face or a desirous look in her eyes. But as quickly as the unguardiness came it vanished, and she would turn to wipe her hands on the apron, clattering dishes or pans or things left in the sink. Karen felt Jud slipping away and still was unable to stop it.

Karen pleaded one day while looking up at him. "You do know I really care about you? Us?"

Jud shrugged, placing both hands in his pockets. "You sure have a strange way of showing it." Then out came his hand and, making a fist, he hit the end table. By catching the edge, it overturned, breaking the vase that held fresh flowers he had brought her.

Karen placed a hand to her mouth to suppress any sound. She was left standing alone while he stalked off to take a long hot shower. Above the water and through the almost-closed door, she heard him yelling at the top of his lungs, "I am tired of playing house! Is anyone listening up there?"

Karen knew he liked hot showers for even the bedroom gold-frame mirror became steamed. His temper was something new of which she was hearing a lot, to the extent he would shut the door so hard it would rattle. At night, they had sometimes taken long walks together, but eventually, he quit asking her to come along and went solo, informing her he needed to clear his head.

The trip had been exciting and painful. During most of the time sightseeing, they would ride the ferry, walk the grounds on Kelly's Island, and look at the lighthouses. It was their downtime and when they were most relaxed. Karen knew there was a great gulf forming between them from her being naïve about how to share completely with him. Things would heat up, but then she found pulling away from him was the only answer. She didn't know what to say, or do, so she did nothing.

One evening after arriving home, he stopped Karen in the kitchen, whispering and breathing heavily on her face. "We need to experiment a little. Let me show you." He caught her arm, and he brought Karen to him with a tight embrace where she felt every inch of him. He began slowly by bending down and lightly but tenderly dropped a kiss. She showed a response by unknowingly parting her lips and lightly urging for more. Again, still not letting her go, he applied a more passionate kiss. Her response was not expected. Her eyes widened while looking at him. She was left speechless and not to mention very stunned. It had been a long time for them to be in contact with one another. She began to feel a real need to respond when he abruptly released her. It was so fast only her leaning against the sink withheld her. Turning quickly with a wide sweep of his hand he pushed the vegetables and containers off the counter, which fell in the double sink and on the floor. His stomping seemed louder than it was when out the front door he went, not even looking back and certainly not taking time to close it.

Karen flung her arm in the air and kicked stuff out of her way. She decided to take a bath. It should calm her down. She jerked the faucet on and slammed down the oil and bubble liquid she was to add. As the water was adjusted to her liking she dropped in the lavender oil. She also added a little lilac salts. She tipped the bubble fragrances and began swirling them in the tub. The light fragrant candles were lit. Stepping into the deep clawfooted tub was such a delight, and she soaked in the hot water with the formed bubbles. She sat for and hour or so and this was her picture of a little piece of heaven. Yes, soaking was awesome and it did much to relax her. The fragrances would carry out into most of the other rooms.

Afterward, Karen would relax on a chaise reading a good mystery. She would settle down with a fresh pot of brewed tea, and only add in one lump of sugar per cup.

But on the evening of a full moon which was one month into their marriage, Karen had gone to the kitchen for a pot of brewed tea, but she had another surprised encounter with Jud. Karen, with eyes closed placed a hand to her mouth and felt the warmth still there from him. She wondered why had he turned and walked out quietly, not saying a word. Anger built, and filled every emotion in her; with her arms in the air she clenched her fists and shook them. Trembling, out loud she screamed, "Even my kisses have no hold on him! What is wrong with him? I don't understand him at all!" Karen was still shaky long into the night.

Not a word was spoken after Jud came back into the house, for she found out the next morning he had not come to bed. Instead, he had chosen to bed down on the sleeper sofa, making no attempt at conversation at all.

Watching Jud through the window of the back door do yard work was both fascinating and painfully agonizing for Karen. Although through the curtains she didn't think he could not see her. She would become almost awestruck. Gazing at his toned body which was bronzed in color, tanned by the sun and wind, sure made her reckless with mental and bodily notions.

Karen knew he usually stashed a shirt in the garage just to slip on should someone come over or in case a need came up to go inside the house. One of the traits she admired of him was his modesty. She knew how he was a confident man. All the looks others gave him only fed his self-image.

Doing physical labor kept him in terrific shape. When he pushed the walk-behind mower, it made his muscles ripple. Karen noticed his long-tailed fingers as they went through his rich brown hair, making it become wavy and devilish, and throwing a chocolate lock forward on his forehead.

Karen brought iced tea out for him and some-times placed her hands in his hair for she could not help herself. Jud would take a step or two backward, placing the fence between them while giving her a wink made her go weak in the knees every time. He moved toward the handle on the mower which was a place to prop his body. While resting and taking a drink, he said, "Thank you. It hit the spot." He gave her a teasing grin with a quick wink. Karen all but fainted, knowing he was enjoying flirting with her but was also keeping at a safe distance.

As a reward at night, she tried to please him by placing relaxing lotion on his back, giving him the best rubdowns she knew how. Once he mentioned, "Your hands feel like hot coals to the touch on my back."

She did this routinely night after night until they lightly kissed, turned over, and said their good nights.

Soon it became impossible for either one to sleep. Jud rolled and tossed all night long causing Karen to awake. In the wee hours, rolling over to her side, he whispered a plea, "I want you, and oh the need."

She willed down her quivering and feigned sleep by pretending not to hear. What was she to do? Her important nightwear had disappeared and her mother had gone on a holiday. She thought she would lay very still for what seemed like forever. She knew if they touched there would be no escape and surrender would come. Karen was never so fright-ened as she was now, even when as a kid lightning struck her parents' house, for she was scared, but this was too close, she could feel his warm breath across her face. Karen just did not know what to do or say and most frightened of his actions. Her worst thought was what if she did not please him? She ached for him deep within, but stayed frozen.

Jud jumped up, slid on his jeans, jamming the zipper, and in a strange voice muttered, "Karen, this is not right—your restraint between us. This is a warning, Karen, take heed. You better fix it." From his clumsy movements, the night stand and the lamp dumped with a crash onto the floor. Again he went outside for a run, not stopping to look back.

Karen was shaken to the foundation. She opened her mouth to shout, "Come back!" But only a tiny sound was uttered.

He kept moving far down the road. Karen could only imagine how angry he was. She had almost given into Jud. The growing lust, desires, wants, and needs were running high, but she must hold out from him. She wanted to hear the three little words, "I love you." This being her first time with a man, she wouldn't settle for anything less; it was all or nothing. It was the answer to trust.

Karen could see Jud was frustrated and angry with the situation their marriage had taken. She knew he had tried to figure out why all the rejection.

Knowing that there had been at least one other woman in his life she saw it was never a problem of his getting his own way. He had gained control over his feelings and managed to offset the anger pent up inside as far as she could tell.

# 6

He raked his hands through his hair a lot, seeing Karen was more perplexing than he ever imagined. Early in the morning, Jud dropped Karen off at her work place at the salon.

Knowing he had time to finish the yard work at home before picking her up from work, he cut his business day short at the bank. He trusted the weather would cooperate and hold off on the rain. It had been three weeks since he had touched the flower beds or did any yard work. His usual hour and a half doing the mowing, weeding of the beds, had taken him almost three hours. Upon finishing the lawn and flower beds, he had become very thirsty, so shirtless Jud went into the house. To his surprise the air was filled with Karen's fragrances. The lilac and Russian sage had been an excellent choice of blend as it rose.

He soon became destitute. His manliness had set in. His nostrils flared. Alertness went all through him and it was new and thrilling. He never thought strongly about using the power of their being married or the weight it carried, but today was different. He felt tautness coming and the excitement in knowing she needed claimed.

Walking into the bathroom he saw Karen relaxed in the tub with big and little bubbles everywhere. How surprising. Karen felt a little worn out after doing just three of her hair customers and she was only one hour and ten minutes into her day.

The shop was without air conditioning since the coolant had run out. The heat had taken its toll. Her day had become way too difficult to try to please anybody. The shop owner had posted a written note at Karen's station a mandatory hair fashion show was scheduled later in the year in another nearby town in which she had assigned Karen to go. It was the latest in hair styling with dry cuts. Normally the news would have excited her, but Karen felt zapped of her strength from the heat.

Karen knew she needed to reschedule her people and she called them one by one. Most of her clients were relieved to stay out of the heated day. Her brow was full of moisture from sweat, and it began to roll down her face. Feeling drained, she decided to take a bus home, thinking she would call Jud later from the house when she was cooled and refreshed.

On the bus, she began to think her low energy level might be from the strange way her body had reacted and felt around Jud lately. The puzzle continued. It's not like he had tried to kiss or touch her, for he hadn't not since the night she pretended to be asleep. Thinking of him made weird and wonderful emotions come alive in her. She felt empty, hurt, and wounded. However, she still ached for him.

Karen had filled the tub with hot water clear to the top. The bubbles were big and inviting. Yes, it was just what she needed to relax. Almost as an afterthought, she knew to call Jud at work to inform him not to pick her up. She decided she would right after the soak. *Plop. Plop.* In feet first she gradually lowered down into the tub. The water was cool, inviting, and so relaxing. Karen felt her eyes slowly close and nothing around her mattered for the moment. Having fallen asleep she woke in a daze, hearing a splash and seeing water all over the floor. Her inwards jumped for joy. She was happy and thrilled to see Jud getting into the tub yet very surprised. Her stomach kept doing flip-flops.

As he gradually sat down and edged closer, he dropped a gentle kiss on her warm enticing lips. Yielding to his response, she returned the kiss, their mouths open and tongues touched.

She felt tingling down to her toes and surely they were moving uncontrollably. Feeling unsure she let a giggle slip out while she pulled on his hair, bringing him closer and breathing out his name: "Jud."

He began lightly touching her slender neck and tender lips, edging with kisses until he reached the fullness of her sweet parted lips. She responded with a touch to his chest. He shuddered from the physical impact. The warmth they generated was compelling. The closeness urged them nearer together until they were lost in her willingness. Together they had climbed new heights with explosions and unknown feelings. In that moment they shared themselves and had become one.

Jud gave a wink while kissing her on the forehead before getting out of the tub. He partly dried off, dressed, and told her a walk was needed. She nodded her head, blushed, and felt weak all over. Every part of her felt elastic. Forcing a rinse off in the shower, she was still in disbelief while drying off and getting dressed. She began weeping for a release and fought to gain control. The feeling in the pit of her stomach was one of uneasiness, and it was upsetting to think of what a great disappointment he must have felt. She thought of what she saw when looking into his green sober eyes. With the lack of experience she knew there was no way of measuring up with the times he had spent with Eurlene. *He needs a real woman more than I could ever know how to be.* In her mind, was the marriage doomed or was there still hope?

She brewed a pot of hot tea and poured it into a cup. She added only one lump of sugar. Going about her business she fixed a snack for them to eat. There was an old saying that stated, "The way to a man's heart is through his stomach" or something like it.

Looking up, Karen implored, *Help us.* Swearing within, she promised never to talk about their earlier event to Jud or anyone! "No, never." It would be as though nothing ever happened.

Jud came into the kitchen upon returning from outside. His eyes were shadowed, and she could not read them. She offered him a plate of finger sandwiches and a tall glass of limeade. She knew he hadn't realized how hungry he had become. She gave a titter, seeing six and a half sandwiches later and two fill-ups of limeade gone. After eating, Jud relentlessly endeavored to give Karen a little peck on the lips. Her head turned as he was leaning in. She continued to walk away and turned on the television.

Karen uttered, "The night is very uncomfortable for both of us."

Jud agreed. "We both are pretty perplexed and need our sleep."

The next day Jud came home with an enormous bunch of flowers. They were her favorite: lilacs, roses, and Russian sage. Karen easily came to tears. He looked puzzled, running his hands through his hair. After placing the cut flowers in a vase they had received as a wedding gift, she ran into his arms, and they embraced for the longest time. Real hope and joy began to sweep through her. Jud just kept caressing her face. She could feel how taut he had become while trying to gain control. Looking into his mystified eyes, and just for a second, she caught a glimpse of raw emotion.

Karen decided to stay busy and schedule as many upsweeps as possible, for not wanting to talk with Jud. She knew they needed space so things could ease back into their old friendship ways. Knowing it was the week of the prom, it wasn't hard to become over booked. Hair arrangements were done in a slick bun or a dreamy French twist. Some even dared to have a basket weave. There was no exception in styles. All occurred throughout the week for the senior girls going to their high school prom. Some received makeup tips also had their nails groomed. Karen had never been so busy. She stayed rushed all week long, working late, well into the evenings.

The salon manager had not seen a week filled with so many young ladies for many years. She herself kept giving a help-ing hand. She washed and dried towels, sterilized combs, and brushes, and wiped down the girls' stations. Work had been so hectic. Each consultant felt going home at the end of their shift had became a real treat. Just soaking their feet was a pleasure.

Karen and Jud fell into a huge boring routine nightly and dinner was mostly casserole dishes. After they washed and dried the dishes, and put them away a little television was watched or music was turned on to cuddle up to while reading a book before turning into bed.

Karen stayed stressed the majority of the time but fell quickly in a twitchy sleep. Her known fact about being pregnant had taken a toll on her. She had an urgency to talk with Jud about the big surprise: the pregnancy. She desired to share her feelings of things, but held off communicating with him for she did not want to be disappointed and grief-stricken by his answers.

Underneath tension steadily mounted between Jud and Karen. Karen began reflecting on a lot of things and people. A period of time had passed, and Karen reached the phone to call Sara. It rang.

"Hello."

"Hi, Karen. Guess what? I'm putting my career on hold and I've decided to be a stay-at-home mom. Ken asked me to consider it."

Karen replied, "You're a natural mom. Go for it." Karen envied Sara and how she loved every minute of being with Timmy and Ken. She didn't seem to mind putting her designing work on the back burner. Karen saw a treasured, loving, and devoted mother.

That night Karen served Jud his dinner. One would have thought the food was chalk. Nothing was really eaten. Karen cleared the table as Jud called his friend Ken. Evidently, he wasn't home, and Jud motioned for her to sit. She was surprised. He spoke freely about his parents. She was glued to the seat so she didn't miss a word.

Jud said, "My parents traveled in certain seasons to promote the bank's programs." He raised his eyebrows. "It was known worldwide. Dad held lectures on branch versatility and mother helped by setting up their display tables when she was available. It's strange, Karen, but both fathers of mine and Ken met during one of the lectures."

Jud told her how a random a brochure on saving and making money had been sent to Ken's father. Karen shifted in her kitchen chair, but kept her hands folded in her lap giving Jud her time.

Jud reached for a cup of coffee. "A great friendship was born between the two men. Jon would try and take in a lecture when time would permit. On one of his trips Jon had brought his son, Ken. Funny, I had also made the trip with my father. We both met on the playground. The keeper of the park introduce us. Ken and I found we had a lot in common."

Karen tried not to wiggle in the chair, but it was uncomfortable. Nothing to her at this point mattered except Jud and what he had to say. She would just have to sit. Jud lit up when he spoke about his friend and family. She saw his jaw relax and his handsome face beckon her on. He told her Ken and he liked playing guitars and jamming to the same kind of music. They enjoyed reading books and attending Sunday services.

Ken, somehow during the summer after the drought, stayed with Jud's parents, and for many more summers to come it seemed. Ken's parents owned a farm in another state. Jon and Sylvia New enjoyed the wide open outdoor space. Idaho had miles of beautiful scenery and wheat fields as far as the eye could see. During harvest time as the sun hit the crops, it looked like they were dripping gold.

Ken was raised as an only child and showed completely different ideas and interests other than farm living. Although he was a natural when working the land, friction developed strongly between him and his father.

Jud overheard his father say what a good friend Jon had become. He wanted to give Ken a safe, secure, and wholesome living with pure values. Tom understood the wandering needs of the News' son.

Jud grabbed his coffee cup. "Ken was a more business-oriented sort of a person, and enjoyed city living. He was mixed with deepen emotions of sadness and happiness from how Tom let Ken stay with their family through the summers without any exchange of money as the years went by."

Jud stood and Karen held her breath, but he was only getting a refill on the coffee. She motioned a time-out with her fingers and took that opportunity to go into the bathroom. Returning she caught Jud's attention and motioned him to come sit in the family room. It was much more comfortable. He could still take her breath away.

Jud appeared relaxed and his five o'clock shadow was peaking on his face. Carrying a fresh coffee and a brewed tea, he came and sat down. Motioning for her to take a cup, he went on. "Ken was obedient in listening to his parents and relied on their instruction. He was not opposed to the plan of sending him off to sharing in the life with Tom. Ken held a great respect for his parents."

Karen took a sip of tea, but sat quietly.

Jud looked over at Karen. "You've read on the drought and its effects in the farmland over the years haven't you?"

Karen gave a simple nod.

"Dad mentioned hard times fell on Jon's farm and the cost of grain and equipment ran high. Ken's parents struggled for a few years before their farm methods began to pay off. What helped was Jon's trade. He was a great carpenter."

Jud smiled. "I visited Jon and Sylvia and saw the chair sets he had completed. He never had any former training, but it looked as though he had been born with a hammer. His pieces were beautiful." Suddenly, he seemed to notice Karen's stillness. "You getting tired, Karen?"

She bunched up her lips. "Not really." She got up and brought a plate of sweets for them to snack on. Jud lifted one and he took two before sitting back down. Crumbs were at the side of his mouth as he spoke. "Sylvia worked with Jon night and day those first years, but she never complained. Sylvia knew how to stretch a dollar and it sure was a good thing. I saw her wait and watch for the sales. She also took in boarders."

Jud shifted. "She wasn't shy in asking people to reduce their price. She had been blessed in knowing how to sew. She darned a lot of socks for her boy and Jon. Most of their clothes were handmade."

Jud had a grin come across his face and his eyes lit up. Karen knew his thoughts were not there. Jud reached for her hand. "Walk with me." He guided her outside, only stopping to get her sweater. "Karen, as boys, we put a band together. We enjoyed singing and playing our guitars. Even though we were good, it still was only a passing hobby. Our names got around, and every once and again we played for a social event." Laughing, he injected, "Though we made very little money, we still had a great time."

The air had a chill. Karen was glad she brought a thermos of hot chocolate. She took this opportunity to talk with Jud about her friend, Sara. Karen handed a slug of warmth for him to drink.

"Jud, Sara had transferred in her freshman year to the high school where I attended. We met in science class where the teacher paired us together for a project to enter into the fair. We found this adventure both fascinating and educational. During this time both of us found each could complete the other one's sentences."

She paused and studied Jud. They sat on the old wooden seat placed in the flower garden. He was slump forward and had lost interest in what she was saying. His manners changed. She quietly stood. His eyes looked spacey before he placed his head in his hands.

Very low in spirits she took the thermos and went inside to the sink. She stood washing the cups and saucers. She locked the doors and saw Jud had gotten up and went to bed without saying anything at all. She thought how she wanted so much to share about their sophomore class and how they decided to try out for the trades program offered in their junior and senior years. The principal had told them it was called "diversified education."

They had to get forms and take tests, but there was a catch. A certain grade point average had to be maintained. Notification for the ones making it into trade class was posted in the neighborhood newspaper two weeks before the eleventh grade began. Karen folding the hand towel remembered how excited and sad they felt as the year ahead left for a separation. Their closeness they would share in their new march of life.

Their junior and senior years were quite a success. At the trade school both enjoyed the subjects they took. Sara began with the home design and Karen chose cosmetology. They each were committed in studying to succeed in their course, but they took time for their friendship also and it continued to blossom.

Karen knew she should be lying down, but she did not want to disturb Jud. She changed into her night clothes and brought covers to the sofa. Karen closed her eyes but did not sleep. She rolled and tossed until her mind went back on the journey about her and Sara.

It was on a Wednesday. Karen and Sara were still attending the reading group. It was six years now. Between her and Sara they had studied or read almost twelve hundred books. They used group meetings to catch-up news or issues that happen during the week. Both tried to resolve each situation before they met for the next reading date.

Sadness entered Karen's chest as she remembered when Sara mentioned she came from a poor family. Her mother had taken in laundry to help make ends meet. Her father had suffered from an old back injury. It surfaced when he was younger working in the mines. His back became weak and as time past he used the wheelchair.

Karen's breathing became deep when she remembered the intense pain she saw in Sara's moist eyes. She tried to comfort her friend and expressed, "He cares."

The girls usually hung out at Karen's house. Her mother always made snacks and had freshly brewed iced tea or lemonade.

One day Sara talked about Ken. How he was twenty-four when he finally moved from the farm. Upon finishing most of his college he again stayed with Jud's family. After he graduated he became a full-time employee as a teller at the bank where Jud worked.

Karen stood, fluffed her pillow and drifted in thought. *Hum, Jud and Ken were always together at Wednesday's reading group. It was just one of their places.* Shaking her head she knew the attraction was mutual between all parties. Her memories brought smiles, chuckles, and even tears.

Karen bowed her head and felt His presence.

*Please guide me and give me wisdom. Thank you.*

Thoughts and sayings of her life's journey flashed so quickly. The morning sun was filtering in and shone brightly on her face. Although nothing was quite figured out, Karen realized how much she loved Jud. One of her answers became clear. She needed to figure out how to better communicate with Jud if she was to save their marriage.

After showering at Sara's, Karen looked into the mirror and patted her tummy. A smile appeared as she was dressing. She knew Jud could make a great father for their child. She was scared, but knew she needed to let him in on the pregnancy. She couldn't keep avoiding him forever.

The looks he shifted her way made her uneasy and reflected he could not tolerate her anymore. Jud had made icy remarks and snarled his lips a few times. Even when he was kind, a November chilliness set in. It always led to either a door slam or the trash would get a kick. This did not count the times he firmly placed a hand on her shoulder or arm to stop her or sidestepped in front of her, bellowing, "Now, listen."

Standing there, she would flinched while waiting for him to speak. He paused for a short moment, and then put his head down shaking it as his feet stomped away. A dead silence fell and nothing more would be uttered it seemed like a long time.

Jud used the excuse of work. It had become old even for her. They never arranged to have any quality time together. They no longer went places, they didn't touch, and kissing had stopped. She began slumping around and was so lonely.

Three weeks had past and things had gotten worst. Karen finally planned to make the first move. It was in the afternoon, and Jud had come home early. She ventured out from the kitchen and was shaking and feeling tumult inside her body. To her, it was a signal, and it would have been easier to walk away.

She placed her fisted hands at her side, gathered a little surge of strength, and pushed forward.

Jud crossed his arms after hitting the counter. "Look, Karen what are you hiding from me?"

"Listen," she growled, pointing her index finger, "I need to tell you something."

"What?" Being impatient, and with his arms flying in the air, he blurted out, "Don't just stand there like a marble statue."

# 7

She straightened her shoulders, forced down her tumbling nerves, and moved a little to the right. She avoided him and pretended to look at the flowers. She faked not hearing him mutter curses. In so doing, Karen slowly turned toward him. "Would you consider playing the guitar tonight?" Again she chickened out from saying what was truly on her mind.

He got to his feet, and the kitchen chair made a horrible sound. Karen placed her hands over her ears. It slid across the floor and knocked over the trash can. Karen placed her hand on his arm but he shook loose and walked outside. Karen tried bracing herself, placing her hands over her ears again, but she could still hear the door banging.

It was late evening before he returned. They didn't attempt reconciliation. There were polite words, but stiffness remaining between them. Karen noticed shadows had appeared around his beautiful green eyes. He seemed tired. He moped, not showing much life. At night, Karen tried to stay awake just to talk and let him know how important he was, but sickness had taken a toll. Waves and heaviness within her stomach and morning or night vomiting caused sleepiness to settle in every time she sit or lay down. Karen tapped her forehead thinking this part of pregnancy was for the birds.

Looking back, she was glad she had gone to Sara's to clear her mind. The escaped was helpful, but still, nothing had been settled. Sara had left a change of clothes for Karen in the bedroom. They once had fit but not now. Karen tried to adjust the skirt and loosen up the blouse, but Karen caught Sara's eye and knew she noticed the change in her figure. Karen bit her lip, but still, she could not tell Sara yet about the pregnancy. She just waved past the door and went to place a call to Jud. She owed him that. She wanted to let him know she was fine and that she had stopped off at Sara's.

He picked up on the third ring. "Karen, I've been worried."

She interrupted. Her voice in her ears sounded shrill and high pitched. "I'm on my way home to talk. We need to clear the air between us." Although shaking, she hoped she sounded braver than she felt.

"Karen." But the line was dead.

Giving Sara a light hug, she promised to call her later. Karen drove toward home. Her head was swimming with all kinds of suppositions. Karen talked out loud. She was building the strength she needed to confront Jud. *What if he refuses to listen or be willing to talk? What if he didn't want the baby or me?*

Karen shivered all the way home. She had rolled the windows up and the heat on low. As if not enough was on her mind the question popped in: What about his parents' divorce? Would it impact them? Her mind went into a whirlwind. Out loud, Karen sighed.

*Oh, how did our life get in such a mess?*

Before she opened the car door, she did a quick review of their situation. She became heavyhearted once again. Her mind went wandering about her parents. They were doing some traveling to a cold state where they were would be trying out a new skill Donald had read from a book. It was on the art of ice fishing. She wished they could be near at this time. Her longing for them put an ache in her spirit. Then the idea of his parents' divorce and them going their separate ways came back to her. She had heard his mother Joan and friend Eli were on holiday and his dad, Tom, was still sorting out paper work from his life with Joan. He wanted to move forward and send everything of hers to the new address she had given him.

Then Karen went over the new fact about herself. She would be unemployed soon, and not able to work, per instruction by doctor's order. Looking up she said, *Now would be a great time for some help.*

As Karen entered the doorway she saw Jud pace and say oaths under his breath. She noticed a new hole in the wall. Jud's eyes were like steel. Then a moan came. It was from deep inside. "Enough is enough." His hands were fisted, and his body was stiff.

She could not believe his temper. It was all Karen could do not to run into his arms. Her need to touch was overwhelming, but again, she willed her hands into fist and to stay by her sides. His rejection would be just more than she could bear.

Karen stepped forward. She took control. She pointed her slender finger. "Do you know what your ways and moods have been like for me?" She didn't wait for an answer. "You, not talking to me, or you, deciding to run from of the house, or slamming things, and now this. Hitting!" She tilted her head and gave a haughty laugh and went on. "You're not the man I want to be around."

Karen took another step. Her voice became pitchy. Jud edged backward. He stumbled and fell halfway into a chair. He looked ghostly.

Karen begun to sweat and became unsteady. She reached out. He made a step toward her. She put her hands to her head. Her eyes rolled backward. She had become light-headed and dizzy before passing out. Karen began to come around and noticed how Jud had managed to kick stuff out of the way while trying to help her. She had seen a jolt, and in two strides, Jud had arrived and knelt beside her. "Karen, Karen wake up!"

Karen moaned. She looked, and there were uncontrollable tears rolled down Jud's face. He began gently rocking her back and forth, stroking her long soft blonde hair. He whispered, "Sweet, pure Karen, I love you."

It was in a low, husky, trailing voice. She wasn't sure of what he had said. Karen only saw his red-rimmed, swollen eyes that caused the ache in her heart to deepen. It had been stabbed through and through. She welcomed his warmth and tried to scoot closer. Her arms slid voluntarily around his neck patting his shoulders then moved to touch his face. Karen hands felt scorched.

He carried her across the room to a wing-side chair. He made sure she was settled before calling the doctor. "The doctor wants to see you." Jud grabbed her sweater and purse, and then slowly helped her into the car.

Karen was like a lamb at the doctor's, quiet and obediently following the nurse. She went into the examining room while Jud stayed and filled out the paper work. Upon finishing he approached the examining room where Karen was sent. He appeared with his lopsided smile, but new lines had crept in and were etched around his beautiful green eyes.

Jud said, "Babe what's the prob?"

But the doctor broke in. "We're transporting Karen to the hospital using the ambulance."

Karen was watching Jud's face when given the news. She could tell he was taken off guard. He looked scared.

At the hospital a nurse with a wheelchair was waiting for her arrival. Jud had followed the ambulance. He once again was caught up in the paperwork scenario.

Karen knew he still didn't know why she was there and certainly he didn't know about the pregnancy. Jud only knew the doctor wanted to run some new test for health reasons, not for the purpose of her and the baby's safety. An order was given for a stay in the hospital. She needed complete bed rest and professional care. She heard steps. In the doorway he leaned in, raked his fingers through his hair, and for a moment seemed stopped. Karen saw his eyes closed and his mouth was moving. She tried to listen as he whispered, "Are you listening?"

Jud stepped into the room "Karen, are you behind curtain number 1 or number 2?"

She realized the amusement in his tone and gave a little giggle, "Silly, I am here behind curtain number 1." Sticking a hand out. "See it's opened." Secretly, she was hoping he wouldn't see the sign, but she saw his eyes look up and knew he noticed a sign saying "Maternity Floor." He had a strange look to him. Karen knew he had questions.

Karen flashed a brave smile. His eyes soften. He winked and returned a strained, lop-sided smile. "This flu or whatever has really taken a toll on you. I'm glad you have professional help to make you comfortable."

He bent to her ear and whispered. "You know I care about you."

Karen knew she was a picture of helplessness. The old mirror was hanging on the opposite end of her bed. Her petite frame robed in a sterile oversized hospital gown and IV's hooked up. She looked into his concerned eyes. He gave her a light kiss on the forehead before straightening up.

Karen felt a little hope at this kind gesture. She gazed at him and smiled. The monitor showed a skipped heartbeat. She felt expectation might be there. Karen experienced the tender and fuzzy notions spreading through her inside. She tried to be positive in her thoughts with the new life created, and also seeing the growing from within, but she feared the unknown. *I really need to tell him the news!*

Jud wished she had been a little glad to see him. Had he misread the signal of the heartbeat on the monitor? He was more confused than ever. He was puzzled over what was wrong between them. He worried how drained and outwardly exhausted she looked. He ran his hand through his hair and wondered how to save his marriage. He could not allow for her to feel trapped. Their marriage seemed doomed.

Jud put on a front, but he struggled going through all the formalities on each shift. He found it was easy being nice to her for a change. In fact, he began seeing to all her needs. Doing so made him feel alive. During that time, Jud felt closer to Karen. He gave and she received everything from him, but the one thing she most longed for was love. He was kind and very considerate.

Jud notified her parents though the ship line. "Donald, Karen has overdone work at the shop and the doctors said she needed complete bedrest. Yes, she's run-down."

Her parents were concerned. "We will be there as soon as special arrangements can be made."

Jud's voice sounded strained and he knew Kate was listening. Her only replied, "Give Karen our love and save some for you."

He called both of his parents one after the other. They expressed their desire for Karen to have a speedy recovery and they warned Jud to slow down. "Son, you sound tired."

He understood they were tied up with rearranged issues of life and it would take some time for them to be freed up.

Jud paused. "I will tell Karen of your concerns, and I do understand." He mostly did not understand them at all, but it looked like he might be headed down the same path. The old saying "The apple doesn't fall far from the tree" seemed to be holding true.

He called Ken and let him know about Karen's stay at the hospital. He asked for coverage in his absence at the bank. He quickly added, "Please let Sara know."

Ken heard Jud give a long sigh.

Jud hesitated. "Ken, there's something I need to talk with you about."

"Anytime my friend. I'm here for you." The line went silent.

Jud checked his memory to make sure yellow roses were one of her favorites. He was glad to know one thing hadn't changed. He saw he had time to place his order and picked up the phone.

Sara came to the hospital not knowing what to expect about Karen. She gathered reading material for her to read. Sara entered the room and lightly touched Karen's arm. "Hi friend."

Karen offered a flat smile.

She could see in Karen's expression that she was hiding something. Sara wanted to know what was going on, but she couldn't pry. She withheld questions out of respect for her friend. Sara instead smiled, sat down, and began to read. She quietly hoped this visit would encourage Karen to get well and rest.

Two long weeks had passed during Karen's stay in the hospital. Jud was glad for her release and to take her home.

"Home," she said. "How good, really good it sounds." Jud had found a need with Karen and it preoccupied his every thought. He did all the fussing about her and enjoyed the time he spent helping, fixing breakfast, making the bed, doing the laundry, or just fluffing a pillow. It puffed up his chest. He would catch her sly glances with her deep blue eyes and it literally sent chills up his spine. She became stronger daily little by little. He began overseeing bank work. He allowed a few hours out of the day.

Two more weeks past. It was evening when he arrived home whistling prepared to fix dinner. He was stopped in his tracks and became weak and pale.

Karen greeted him with "Surprise." She took his hand, and a wonderful meal was waiting. He held her out from his arms and saw that she was outright stunning. Karen wore a new gold low-cut, free-flowing dress. She was breathtaking. He had never seen her look so beautiful. She wore just a hint of makeup that graced her faced. Karen was more appealing than any model he had ever seen or dated. He felt giddy, just like a school kid being caught in the candy jar, looking and wanting her all at the same time.

Jud began to bead with sweat and went into a panic attack. He quickly lost his tie, unbuttoned his shirt, and took off the rust colored jacket. He gave her a kiss and instantly withdrew. His hand flew to his forehead. His uncontrollably displayed behavior made him feel sad. Karen had sent unknowing signals, and he again was only thinking of his physical need. Shaking his head, he realized she would no longer need him. He shuffled into the bedroom, and his face dropped significantly. Sadness set in. Sitting there he would seek out the attorney and have him draw up the papers and set her free.

Early the next morning he stopped at Ken's house and offered him a lift into work. On the way he confided in Ken about a plan to let Karen out of their loveless marriage. "It's just lust between us."

Ken took a second look at Jud.

"I love her, but it's not shared or returned. She treats me like I have the plague. There is no pleasing her anymore. It's more perplexing than I imagined." Jud gave a heavy sigh. The lack of honor he felt came straight from Karen.

"We are not like most people, Ken. Our love play is very limited. I have these up-close natural feelings we get so far exploring our needs, then she stops. She won't answer questions. She flings her hand up in the air or says stop. Pal, I get angry and walk away. Ken, what's wrong?"

Ken closed his jaw. He seemed shocked and was staring at Jud in a most unusual way. He stumbled for words of wisdom and evidently couldn't find any. Moments passed. Ken let out a long breath. "Jud, it sounds like lack of communication. Understanding is needed. You need to say what you're thinking and feeling. Do this with Karen behind closed doors—soon. Talk with your wife like we talk, as best friends."

In the afternoon, Ken, being concerned, placed a call to Sara. He told her to pray. "Jud has possible plans of divorcing Karen."

Sara stuttered. "Why? I've never heard Karen say anything about being unhappy. You know she is exceptionally closed-mouthed, but I will pray."

On the ride home, Ken let Jud know what Sara had told him. Jud raked his hand through his rich chocolate hair and rode in silence. He did a lot of thinking.

Serious thoughts came about Karen. He waved to Ken as he drove off. Jud pulled over and stopped the car. He dropped his head and pounded the steering wheel. At that instant he decided on a quick trip to see his father. He travel for another hour then stopped at a roadside phone. "Hello, Karen."

"Jud?"

"I'll be home tomorrow late. Some business came up. I'm headed for Dad's. I just called so you could go ahead with your plans."

"Thanks. You be careful."

"What? I will be."

Hanging up the phone, Jud felt like yelling. But instead, he hit the door and muttered. "I just don't get it. Why is she so impassive with me?"

The phone rang. Karen thought it was Jud again. "Hello."

"Hi, Karen, is it all right to bring Timmy and come over for a visit?"

"Sure."

"I was wondering if there's anything you would like to talk about? I'll listen."

Karen tossed her head about. "No not really, but come on over."

The doorbell rang, and Karen gave Timmy a kiss and handed Sara a glass of iced tea. During their time together, only small talk was made. Karen enjoyed playing with Timmy, making animals sounds and rolling a ball as usual, although no lifting was done. Karen swished in her clothing as she moved about. She saw Sara staring. "So do you like my new look?"

Smiling. "Well, your style has changed for sure. It's no longer form-fitting. It's cute though long and baggy. What's with the hat?"

Karen sighed. Fingering the flower on top with raised eyebrows and hands, she flipped the pedals but said nothing.

Karen kept her appointment with the doctor. It was a follow up. "Karen, everything has checked out fine for you and the baby. Call me if you have any concerns or see you next time."

The problem had been a vitamin deficiency. How silly she felt for not even thinking about needing vitamins. Thoughts of Jud played heavy on her heart and nettled her mind while he was away. She hoped the visit with his father would give him some answers.

At the doctor's office, Karen read a brochure left from the reading group about a reasonable getaway. It gave her a brilliant idea. Jud and her should take a trip, maybe go to Lake Erie for a weekend. They could ride the ferry and see Kelly's Island. Since they would be away from everyone, friends, work, and phones, perhaps they would have a discussion or two.

Karen hurriedly called and made the arrangements. Excitement was in the air. New hope had leaped forward in Karen's heart. The trip would be for an afternoon, an evening, and a day. Karen called Sara to come over. Within minutes, Sara arrived. She mentioned the plans to Sara with glee in her eyes.

Sara replied, "I think it's good. You both should get away. I hope this trip works out all your differences. I know you are having troubles, my friend." Sara bit her lip. "My prayers are with you." Unexpectedly the words came rushing out. "I heard the news about Jud possibly wanting a divorce."

Karen choked on a chocolate chip cookie and Sara began pounding on her back.

Suddenly the front door opened. "Hello." Jud swaggered into the room, giving her a lop-sided smile which showed his deep dimple.

Karen blurted, "I have made weekend plans for the both of us."

Jud leaned over and picked up the suitcases in the hall. "Is this all?" He looked over his shoulder. "Let's go." Glancing at Sara, he ordered her to lock up for them when Ken got there.

Jud looked at Karen, and she wore a blush. He knew her personality had changed lately but he pretended not to notice, and he didn't say anything about her size difference or style.

Sara stood there with her mouth gaping wide open and waved. Karen looked out the rear window long after they were out of Sara's sight.

The radio was playing low in the car. Different oldies were being selected. Karen reached in the back seat for a scarf while placing her hat on the floor mat, when she saw his guitar. Memories came flowing to her mind. She heard Jud humming. She listened and soon joined in. They were having a great time singing and laughing. Their time went by quickly as they traveled.

# 8

Karen noticed Jud's jaw had dropped and how relaxed he seemed. The once-lined face was now very structured. It had been a long time for her to see him like this, and yes, it was very refreshing.

She heard his stomach growl as he turned a little to the right. "Karen, you hungry?"

She touched his tanned hand. "I'm starved." They made their stop at the roadside café and ate grilled cheese sandwiches, pickles on the side, with iced tea before boarding the ferry.

Jud seemed happy and was outgoing. He took Karen's hand as they walked to the front side of the ferry. He suggested she hold onto the rail.

A horn blew as they looked into each other's eyes. It brought a new promise to both of them. New excitement crackled in the air.

A surprise breeze came and brought an amazing splash of the lake's water. It sprayed them heavily. They laughed. Jud and Karen were having a wonderful time when she felt movement. Oh, it was the baby. She placed her hands where she felt movement but quickly released them. She looked to see if anyone had been watching. Karen had not realized this had become a habit. Jud had followed her hand movement, but he seemed to be distracted.

A gust of wind came from nowhere, and a hat passed by. He reached out and caught it. Smiling, Karen saw how truly gorgeous he really was. The people on the ferry clapped as he bowed. Karen just started chuckling.

Now Karen and Jud's eyes met. She could see in his facial expressions he was taking in her looks. He reached for her face. "Karen, you're glowing. You have this beauty."

Karen went to speak, but the communication bell rang and the ferry docked. She saw a sign held up for them and nudged Jud as she pointed. They waved to the older couple and joined them. They followed being only steps behind. She noticed the older couple holding hands. Karen swayed into Jud, thinking how nice it was that they were still in love after all that time.

Karen was beaming and glad the reading group had run this travel special. It was a cost-saving plan; plus it would allow time for them to really rediscover one another. At least, Karen hoped and prayed it would.

Jud and Karen were shown their cottage and given the schedule of events to attend. They both agreed it was awesome. First was free time. Karen chose to read and rest while Jud went for a walk.

Jud wanted to know more about this intriguing place Karen insisted they stay. The air was so clean and pure. He noticed breathing was done without difficulty. The sulfur from sub-city living was not present. The grounds were lushes green, and the cascading sound of water inviting. It became enchanting, like an emerald, beckoning him closer. He felt welcomed by the island, and a nearness to a higher level.

Jud peeked into the room and saw Karen had changed into a cute red and yellow striped sundress.

"Is this a new dress? You sure look pretty." He didn't wait for an answer. He grabbed a quick shower, pulled on a crispy, white pocket T-shirt with a pair of khaki pants, slipped on his sandals, and carried a corduroy suit coat. His aftershave lotion of musky spice mingled with the air. It made Karen very aware of his maleness and Jud's relaxed posture. Karen became very much alive.

She picked up her sweater and clipped it around her shoulders. They walked to meet with the older couple. They followed the steps of the eerie stone path down to the dinner hall. After eating the prepared meal of beef sandwiches, served with tomato soup, and iced tea, they went to a reading group and listened to the after-dinner speaker, Mr. Life. He talked on building trust with one another whether it was with a business, friendship, or in a marriage. The key was to be honorable in all things, beginning with open communication, through prayer, to the other party.

Near the end they sang a few songs and some shared a story or two before free time took place. The clock tick-tocked and did not stand still; soon they would be turning in for the evening. Time was fleeing by quickly.

Jud gazed at Karen. "How about taking a stroll with me?"

He took her hand, clasping her other one over it. "Sure. Jud, I'm enjoying our time together."

Jud shot her a puzzled look. Karen slowly began to talk. He saw her nervousness, but couldn't get a single word in edgewise so bending she felt his breath near her lips. She looked surprised as he gave her a little kiss. She became quiet.

In the private stillness of the night, he had planned to talk about their possible separation. He had hoped they could at least still stay friends in parting. How he had wanted them to stay together forever and had not wanted them to end up like this. Softly in a whisper and bowing his head he said, "Are you here? Will you listen?"

As their lips touched, sparks from their inner warmth drew them closer and closer together. He was probing at her parted mouth. They embraced closer, both feeling his need. She put her arms around his waist and squeezed.

His maleness was sinking fast. He needed distance to gain self-control. Hesitating, Jud pushed himself away. He reached for her hand, walked quickly, and led them forward on the trail. His legs felt so heavy they just wanted to buckle under him. Again, his willpower had almost faltered as they continued in quietness.

Glancing around, they had made their way to the isolated part of the beach. Karen's hands flew to her mouth as she gasped and looked at Jud. He had dropped his clothes and ran into the water. "He's buck naked."

She held her hands to her mouth. She was so surprised and did a nervous laugh. Mentally she had pictured him in the buff many times, but physically he was so conservative and restricted when she was around. Karen spread out his suit jacket and deciding to sit down, she slipped off her shoes to play toesy in the warm sand.

She watched Jud float then swim. He looked like a dolphin, showing ownership of the waters surrounding him. It made her feel like a kid opening a present the night before Christmas and being caught. Still staring, Jud saw her and waved his hand. He beckoned her to come. Looking around she saw they were in total darkness, except for the moonlight. Without hesitation she went in the water. She left only her panties and bra on.

The moon gave off many illusions. There were shadows and shapes lurking about, but no one was there but them. For a moment, it seemed, as if they were caught in a different dimension and a forgotten place. A dimension in which Karen would mentally reflect upon the future days with the purpose of secretly knowing how much she loved Jud. She became tired, but being with him gave her energy and nothing else matter. She had new hope. It was time to tell him about their baby.

Jud glanced and thought her breasts looked fuller and her body rounder. He really did not know what to think, except for the moment at hand that mattered most because she was there with him. They had swum for quite awhile and played. Both splashed and dunked each other. Jud at one point took a hit, for she double-dunked him unexpectedly. He didn't see it coming. They frolicked for a long time in the water.

When they came to shore, the moonlight was hidden behind the clouds. Every once in awhile the moon would peek from a cloud and stream light across their faces. As they got dressed, nothing was said to the other.

Heading back to the cabin, it was only natural to entwine his hand in Karen's. The touch sent jolts to the depth of his stomach. He paused and dropped a few kisses on her tender, willing lips. *I'll talk with her later.*

Could this be a new beginning? It seemed promising of more to come. He felt her willingness. Either love was in the air, it was a magical night, or maybe even answers were forthcoming. At the cabin he hurried and showered the lake water from him. He didn't want to use all the hot water.

Karen fixed peanut butter and jelly crackers from the mixings she had brought from home, just in case she had the urge to eat again. At that thought, a smile beamed across her face. Jud came out just in time to catch her smile. He was dressed, but his hair was devilishly damp.

He reached for a couple of crackers his muscles rippled. "Good idea you brought along the jam and peanut butter." He ate and smiled while patting his tummy.

Karen was amused. She turned to take a warm shower. While the water cascaded over her, thoughts came of how she missed the tub. The shower just could not replace her comfort of soaking. It was not the same. Being brave, Karen graced the room without makeup and shyly crooked her index finger, motioning him to follow her.

Jud stood by the bed. His eyebrows arched as they locked eyes. He brushed her lips and she quivered. Her velvety shoulder-length hair swayed making her blue eyes sparkle. Her hair smelled sweet and fresh. The dampness held him.

Karen was on her tiptoes and kissed his cheek. They were only inches apart. He placed his arm around her and drew her nearer. "Kitten, you are beautiful." They hugged. She shivered then he trembled as an undercurrent flowed. He twirled her hair, and with raised eyebrows, he said, "Karen, shall we?"

Her shyness stood between them. He kept her with his arms.

She whispered, "Maybe." She felt his abs move. Jud bent and kissed her passionately.

Jud heard someone say, "I love you." But who, he wondered, while looking around the room. He placed his hand over his mouth and realized it had come from him. Had he said it out loud? His heart had changed. When had she slipped through? He was stunned.

She looked into his wide eyes. He took her by the hand, walking backward toward the bedroom door. His eyes twinkled never leaving hers. He took his foot and shoved the door closed. She sighed.

He touched her arm and something moved. Jud's eyebrows formed into a question. Jud took a step apart, but placed his hands on her face. Karen blushed. Still pink, Karen placed her hand over his and half-smiled. "Jud, you're going to be a father."

Sitting up. "How did this happen? When? I need to know."

Karen's breathing was calm. "First, I want to say I'm glad the secret is out. I feel a flood of relief." She closed her eyes. *Thank you for listening.*

He touched her arm and tried clearing his throat. Karen saw his mouth open, but no words came out.

Being somewhat silly, she began. "Jud, you remember my very first time with you?" Looking puzzled, Karen went on, "Hello, it took place at home in the bathtub. Well, it left lasting telltales." She grinned and choked out, "It sure turned out to be more than a nice, rich soothing bubble bath." Throwing her head back, she gave another hearty laugh. Rolling out of bed, she slipped back into her clothes.

Arising, Jud got dressed and had an instant urge to console Karen. He noticed the deep blushing even more the nearer he came to her. He saw how beautiful and wanton she'd become.

She was so desirable. Holding out his arms, she went willingly. He wanted to protect her from any harm or hurt. Mixed feeling swelled up inside him. As Karen nuzzled against his chest, he felt her surrender and his defeat.

Jud's innards quivered. His anger escalated as he slipped on his running shoes. He pushed harder, faster, on his daily run. His arm jabs pierced the air. Sweat dripped from his brow and his body was clammy. Moisture flew as he shook his head. He was furious with his self-centeredness. How could he have been so recklessness and unprotected. He would never live this down. How insensitive he was taking advantage of Karen while in the tub. He was a real jerk and used barbaric methods. Terrible actions.

Doubling over, he tried to breathe. *Look at this mess. It's just my luck she got pregnant—her first time.*

Shaken to the core, he had let his hormones take over and follow his own lust. It was a weak moment of self-pleasure and a lifetime of consequence. He sat down and held his head between his legs. The news of their creating life changed things. Jud knew his proper place was now with Karen and their unborn child. He had been raised with strength of character and honor. He was determined to take responsibility and step up to the plate. He would make their marriage work. Looking at Karen how had he not known? Pregnancy became her. She radiated, her skin glowed.

The next day Jud got up early and prayed. *Help me and give me wisdom.* When he returned, he lightly kissed Karen. "Hi beautiful." A smile came across his face as he said, "Get dressed, sleepyhead, so we can continue on our schedule. The tour starts in one hour. It's the lighthouse. I heard it has been turned into a museum."

He wanted to buy Karen a special souvenir for he knew her fondness of this place. He also needed to re-evaluate these new feelings he was developing for her and consider what would be next for them.

Karen slightly smiled. "Be right with you. I'll grab a quick shower."

Hand in hand they followed their tour guide. Jud lean to her ear. "Stay with the group. I'll be right back." He kissed her lightly on the cheek.

Peering in the gift shop he decided on a necklace holding a miniature lighthouse. He caught up with her and continued their tour. They stopped and listened as the guide pointed out how the lighthouse changed over to a museum.

The matronly woman spoke. "It became dangerous for the viewers taking trips to the lighthouse. The island people wanted safety for them and the tourists. The community held a meeting and the museum idea passed."

The guide began walking, but Jud reached for Karen and stood firm. Looking into her puzzled eyes he held up a wrapped package. She brightened up reaching her hand out for the bag. It was a charm. A tear dropped from her face.

"I'm getting you a white gold chain when we get back to hold the lighthouse piece."

"Okay." Biting her lip, she touched his chest. "Jud, our being here together is what I think is most important."

Jud guarded his emotions. He took her hand and walked the path to the rocky side. "Karen, close your eyes." Carefully he sat her down making sure her eyes were still closed "Surprise." There waiting was a picnic lunch. He began strumming the guitar.

Her eyes opened and she clapped. Tears began to fall down her face, but she looked absolutely ecstatic.

Gazing at her that very moment, without a doubt, he knew there would never be any mention of a divorce. The secret and the march of life went on from there for both of them. They enjoyed themselves with the food, beverages, and songs he provided. Karen wide eyes showed appreciation of his time and effort he had put forth. "Jud, you've made this trip perfect, positively perfect! More than I had ever hoped for." She had folded her hands and appeared to be praying.

He momentarily looked one more time at her as they docked and said their good-byes to the older couple. They both hugged and waved to the other couple as far as they could still see them.

Jud marveled at Karen's beauty. She always was easy on the eye, but this was different. It went deeper.

One evening, Karen was brushing her hair and looked into the mirror. She noticed her hair appeared longer. Putting the brush down, she tapped her fingernails, and they seemed harder. She beamed. Her new role of motherhood was one she really relished.

Karen became incredibly devoted to Jud and the unborn child. She placed sweet nothings in his lunch pail. They would be with his cookies or on top of his peanut butter sandwiches. Karen wanted to move into a larger place before the baby came. She had asked Jud, but it did not happen.

One evening Karen called Sara. "Is it all right for me to come over? You're not in the middle of anything are you?" And she giggled.

The doorbell rang, and Ken greeted Karen and waved her in. Karen sat in the kitchen with her friends talking and catching up. Karen couldn't hold it in any longer.

"I have great news. Jud and I are pregnant."

Clapping, Karen looked at Sara. Sara looked at Ken, gave him a peck, and then flew into Karen's arms. Before the evening was over, the three prayed a note of thankfulness as they stared toward the stars.

Jud had met with Ken the day Karen and he had returned from their holiday. He had told him the news about Karen and the baby but swore him to secrecy. It was a man's code.

He told Ken even how it happened. "It certainly wasn't planned." Jud shook his head and walked Ken outside the bank. "Ken, you know how our work here was caught up...Well, I left early that Monday and hurried home to play catchup in the yard. Oh, the sight the back garden was in. It was pitiful. It had been three weeks since mowing or weeding. The yard was shaggy and weeds had overcome the flower beds.

"I looked at the sky and a dark cloud was overhead. The leaves were turning inside and out. The radio was on and a weather man predicted pop-up rains. So I pushed the lawn mower and moved with intensity. I had just finished the beds and the yard when the first drops began. I glanced at the time and hurried inside the house. I wanted to wash up before getting Karen at her work place. But when I checked the answering service, she hadn't called."

Jud hung his head. Ken placed his hand on Jud shoulder. "Jud, don't be so hard on yourself."

"Ken." Tears were in his eyes. "But scented fragrances floated past my nose before I finished washing my face and hands." Jud gave a long sigh. "I went wild. I reached the bathroom, and there she was, the total package. The tub water was running and bubbles were everywhere. She was soaking and had her big toe in the faucet."

Rubbing his chin, he stopped. "I tried to control my feelings, but my clothes went into a heap and into the tub I went. Ken, the rest is history." His hands waived wide in the air. "With her in my arms, it made me feel like a giant nine feet tall. I was the luckiest man alive to be on this planet. She left a burning effect on me. I smoldered."

Ken again patted Jud on the shoulder while nodding in perfect silence.

# 9

During the weeks that followed, Karen was either at Sara's or they called each other daily. Karen tried to visualize mental lessons of Sara's care for Timmy. She watched different issues arise, whether it was toys or feeding or nap time. Karen pondered if she should let Sara know how she became pregnant. She knew the subject would not be mention by Sara. Karen was still keeping secrets and found her situation too personal. She felt embarrassed. Karen dried her hands and a smile came. She was glad things were better between her and Jud since the trip. She noticed little things changing.

Jud had always been an early riser, but looking out their bedroom window at six AM she noticed his car was already gone. A note on the nightstand read, "I'll be late getting home. I didn't want you to worry."

He came home after dark. She tried to keep his meals warm, but they were usually dried out. Sara rang Karen. "Hello."

"Karen, I feel something is wrong between you and Jud."

Karen tried to speak, but Sara over spoke her. "You need to know Ken's watching Jud resume his work load. Jud has taken on all new clients and staying busy."

Karen let out a long gasp. "Thanks friend, but it's going to be all right. Just pray."

Bank promotions were given, and Jud received one right after another until he made CPO. He held a high image. Karen watched Jud obtained a yearly gym pass. He said, "It was to meet potential new clients."

He exhibited a new line of men's clothing and even had his teeth whitened. Karen saw how his nearly straight teeth glistened. Jud's photograph was posted on the side of buses. He was most photographic. Women no matter their age turned their heads and some unmercifully flirted with him.

It didn't matter knowing he was married. They didn't care. He was so charismatic, tall, and handsome.

Karen pretended not to notice his withdrawal from home or her. When thoughts began, she would shush them away. She was madly in love with Jud, and they would work things out. She simply needed to be patient and enjoy what time they had as a couple.

Donald called Jud at the bank. "Hi, son, can you reserve a cottage in the villa for Kate and me? We should be there next week."

Jud let out a long sigh, and he hit his forehead with the palm of his hand. Great! Karen's parents were coming for a visit. "Sure I'll get right on it."

They ended their conversation and Jud made the necessary arrangements. He rented a small cottage in the villa for Karen's parents to stay in. He thought how their place was becoming too small and how it would be getting smaller with the baby.

He played the perfect host. He was so debonair, witty, and attentive with Karen and family. He would give her a brief touch on the lips, and she would pale.

As they were eating breakfast, Kate looked over at Karen. "Let's go shopping. I'll call Sara and see if she can come."

Kate drove into the city. The three ladies talked about everything from the nice weather to the fashion's color being red and splashy. Kate found a parking spot and they walked. Sara and

Karen were only too happy to catch Kate up on the hometown news and gossip.

Karen turned to her mother while Sara tried on clothes. "You know the beauty shop scheduled me to attend a hair class! I have to go. Mom, will you come? I'd need you to help drive the distance. Okay?"

Kate checked her purse for her and Donald's schedule. She looked into Karen's eyes. "I'll need to talk with your father. I'm not sure on how long we are staying, but I'll let you know—soon."

Donald cornered Jud as he and Ken finished talking. "Let's go golfing. You still have your clubs, Jud? Ken?"

Jud tried to stall, and Ken smiled. "We do and that would be great."

Donald, Ken, and Jud had always gotten along. Donald gave a hushed laugh for he never liked golfing. He could hold his own, but he really enjoyed the great outdoors and walking. Jud and Ken, on the other hand, were great golfers. Jud didn't participate in any tournaments, but Ken had.

Donald shook his head observing Ken's ponytail. Never at work. That would be a no, no. As the men played Donald didn't know what kept Ken from burning to a crisp. His ivory skin-tone was blotchy. Jud was getting darker. Glancing at Ken he saw a very laid-back person taking his time to putt. On the other hand, Jud was very energetic and was not relaxing. In between holes, Jud would have one hand in his pant pocket, rattling something, and his footwork was always on the move.

The men declared Ken the winner after their eighteen holes. They had promised the ladies they would join them, and went to shower and change clothes. They saw the ladies who waved and caught up with them. The men were amused but said not a word as they watched their ladies ooh and ah over every baby item they saw or picked up in the stores. As they were leaving, Donald nodded at the hotdog vender standing at the corner. The six stopped and ate heartily.

Kate had Karen register at the local department store for baby things. She also had arranged for a baby shower while she was still in town. The following week and a half, many people came to the shower. Some people attending were acquaintances of Karen's parents from the business world or club friends. Sara was in charge of the games, and she also served little cakes with pink and blue booties.

Karen received many things for the baby, more than she would ever need or would be used. The baby outfits and blankets were either in a mint green or a pastel yellow. Everything seemed to blend or match.

A few days passed and Donald with Kate arranged for Ken, Sara, Jud and Karen to dine out for an evening dinner, which was rare. Jud had to leave a little later, so he drove separately. Ken rode with Donald. Kate drove the rented vehicle and took Sara and Karen.

At the restaurant, they waited until their names were called. Donald stepped forward. "I'm waiting on three other members to join us."

The host smiled and was about to call the next person on the list when Kate waved. "Yoohoo, Donald." He smiled shook his head as he acknowledged Kate. Donald took Kate's arm. "We're all here now."

The men were in for quite a surprise. Kate had bought Karen a most daring red maternity outfit. The top had tiny, slender straps crossing over her bare shoulders. The neckline had a peek-a-boo appearance, drawing the eye to the deep plunging front. It accentuated Karen's enhancements. Her skirt had a split on the right side, showing off a great angle of her well-curved leg. She wore pointed shoes in a matching red with a four-inch heel.

Sara stepped forward wearing a great Daisy Mae dress. It had a scooped neckline with attached puffy sleeves. The top had darts to the waist that accentuated the smallness of Sara's waistline. The skirt was extremely full and swished as she walked. Donald arched his brow in a given way, as he whispered something to Kate and squeezed her hand. She automatically tossed her head back and gave a quiet tittering laugh.

Jud turned red when he tripped at the archway. Straightening, he whistled and clapped with hands overhead as Karen entered the room. He looked at Kate and returned her smile. Heads turned as they walked by. Kate knew Karen was extremely stunning and sophisticated. It showed in Jud's eyes. Her pregnancy did not look out of place, and as a matter of fact, it made her all the more appealing. Even Ken let out a low whistle.

When Sara entered, she held up a hand and glided over by Kate. Ken beamed all over himself. He slithered over and leaned to Sara's ear. "You are beautiful. Sara, I'm so proud to be your husband."

Sara blushed as Kate patted her back.

Jud smiled and made the walk over to Karen. He placed an arm positively around her shoulders and to the world said, "You are the wow factor, Karen!" Blushing, she raised her head and deepened her smile. She looped her arm around his waist and gave him a slight pat on the back.

Kate folded her hands and smiled at her success. She was trying to keep the significance alive between Jud and her daughter. She knew Karen loved Jud with all the heart and soul.

Their dinner was wonderful at the county diner. The tables were laid with blue tablecloths and chicken candle holders. Everyone ordered the country fried chicken with slaw and butter potatoes. Portions served were like truck drivers ate.

Now the diner was known for their apple pie a la mode. Being full, they each took a piece of the pie with them as they left and parted for the evening. Ken and Sara thanked everyone. Sara smiled at Kate.

Jud took Karen's arm after a group hug. "We had a great time. Thank you." He hugged Kate and shook hands with Donald again.

The next day Donald met with the realtor. He was taken aback when presented with a list of to-do things before the showing scheduled in one month. He looked at the list in disbelief and waved his arms in the air. *Help!*

Nathan told Donald about Karen's visit to the house. "Karen stayed long after I left. But not before she also said she wanted to come back for another visit before the house sold."

Donald said nothing but pondered on what he was told. He closed his eyes for a brief moment. He envisioned Karen riding her blue bike up and down the driveway ringing the silver bell, while playing bus ride. She carried little pebbles using them for money. He switched his thoughts to a time when the pony, Lumps, pulled a single-seat cart in which she enjoyed guiding. At times, she would just ride Lumps' bare back.

A drop of rain hit Donald's forehead causing his eyes to open. Arms across his chest, he finally visualized all her friends around the big weeping willow in the backyard, taking turns swinging on the tire swing. Listening, he could almost hear her laugher.

Donald, in quiet mode, nodded to Nathan. "Yes, as a family we were definitely happy living here."

One evening as Donald and Kate were walking as they often did, he mentioned the to-do list. He advised her it needed done before they could sell the house. "Kate, will you make the draperies for the house one more time?"

He saw Kate beam while shaking her head.

"I don't want any store-bought ones. Never liked them!"

Kate placed a hand up. "Tss, tss, Donald. Rest assured I'll take care of them."

"You knew I went to Mr. Spencer's office before driving to the house?

"Yes."

"Kate, I found out Jud had seen him also. I don't know what it was about, though. I hope it was business's sake, not Karen's."

Karen's parents had set up a surprise fund for her twenty-sixth birthday. There was just one clause: she had to be settled in a happy marriage, with family or planning one.

Donald and Kate kept an eye on Jud and his ways. Thoughts of why Jud saw Spencer, the attorney, kept bothering them.

Karen finally looked at all the shower gifts. She had received a hand-carved rocker from Jud's dad. He left a note, evidently knowing she would enjoy rocking the baby when it was born. Karen marveled at how grand it was in every way. On the note, it said, "Had you in mind while whittling."

Jud's mother sent a $150 gift card. Karen gasped. It was a huge amount of money. She knew it would come in handy. Her parents bought a beautiful white bassinet. It came with everything: a pillow, tiny sheets, leak pads, the entire blanket group one would ever need, and of course, everything that was in the shade of delicate pink. Kate had told her, "I just know it is going to be a girl."

Jud and she were amused with Kate's determination as they squeezed each other's hand.

There were baby bottles of plastic and glass. Diapers (both cloth and disposable), toys of rattles, squeaky bears, and puppies. There were onesies of green and yellow shades and also lots of blankets of different sizes. Sara had taken down the names and gifts so Karen could send out the thank-you cards with reflection.

Before Tom and Dora, his new wife, left town, Donald and Kate asked them out to dinner. They drove to a fish fry in southern Ohio and stuffed themselves. It was an all-you-could-eat buffet. Dora and Kate ate fish and chips in a basket with a piece of homemade peach pie. The ladies remained at the picnic table talking while the men went for a brief walk.

Tom wanted a private talk with Donald and nudged him to walk toward the creek. Tom didn't want to take a chance of being over heard. Tom stated, "Jud came for a quick visit. He was confused about Karen's feelings toward him. He mentioned Karen and he were not getting along. He implied they may even get a divorce." Tom, shook his head and went on. "Out of concern, I've watched them. I think Jud has dismissed the idea of divorce, and I guess they decided to work things out."

Donald just shivered. "Tom, I wonder if Jud really ever loved Karen, or do you think he was just playing her along to make him look good in the community?"

"Donald, while Jud visited he was sincere and spoke of his love for your daughter. And I think he loves her. It looks like maybe he's a little confused right now."

The men motioned for the ladies to join them. Kate arm-punched Dora. "Look." Both admired the quilts made by the village ladies.

As they were leaving, the ladies showed their husbands the prices pinned on the quilts. The men spoke about how impressed they were with the sale prices.

Ken invited Jud and Karen over for the evening, and they built a bonfire. Sara arranged chocolate graham s'mores to fix. Jud came, carrying the guitar over his back. Karen made fluttery eyes at Jud as they walked hand in hand. As the s'mores was settling, Jud challenged Ken on the guitar. Halfway through, Ken came from the house, jamming. Karen punched Sara laughing. Soon all four sang. Time quickly slipped away and was into the wee hours.

"Jud, it has been way too long since we have gotten together and jammed. We must do this often," Ken said.

Jud nodded as he slung his guitar over his shoulder. "Soon my friend."

Karen reached for Sara as she got up from the log. Both girls clapped.

Jud looked at Ken. "Thanks for a great night and for caring my friend."

The next day, everyone said their farewells and went their separate ways. Tom and Dora went home to Mississippi, and Donald with Kate went on another adventure, traveling the Mediterranean Sea. Jud and Karen were tired and simply went to bed.

Early the next morning, Jud arose quietly, hoping not to awaken Karen for he wanted to surprise her. He heated the water for her tea and began fixing breakfast. The eggs, bacon, and toast were placed on a tray with flowers from the yard, all of which was carried to her.

Hearing her name, she gasped in surprise. Then she slowly smiled.

Jud was occupied with her inner and outer beauty while setting down the breakfast tray. Karen stretched, arching her body and making it look very tempting. Her breasts were at a high rise. Jud cleared his throat and made an excuse and hurriedly left the room. He muttered incomprehensibly in a soft voice, "This is about pleasing her, not me. What is wrong? Why do I sometimes have this struggle?" Jud directed his eyes upward. *Are you listening?*

Jud returned and looked lovingly to Karen. "Listen."

"I don't hear anything."

"Great. I wanted some alone time with just you. Finally, we can put the baby gifts away."

He willed himself to stay in control, checking himself often. He flirted with Karen all day and noticed how considerately more comfortable and relaxed she became around him. Jud was pleased. They placed all the baby clothes in a dresser and all but the last blanket was put up. Jud stepped outside to enjoy a breath of fresh air and asked Karen to join him.

She answered, "I will. I'm going to put the last blanket up. I'll try the top shelf."

The phone rang. Laying the blanket down, Karen shuffled over and answered the phone; it was for Jud. "May I take a message and have him call you back?"

The woman gasped at the other end. "It's rather urgent I speak with him."

"Wait just a moment, please." She laid down the phone and called out the door. "Jud, you're wanted on the phone." The door closed behind her as she waited tapping her foot. "You coming?"

Jud smile and touched her lips as he headed for the phone.

She didn't give much thought of who might be on the other end, except that it was a little unusual for him to get a business call at the house. Shaking her head, she lifted the baby blanket and placed it on the shelf.

Jud turned back and kissed Karen on the nose then stepped forward, picking up the phone. Karen daringly winked at him, turned, and headed toward the bathroom. She turned on the water and prepared for a shower. Her cheeks were still flaming hot and red-looking in the mirror. Inwardly, she admitted flirting was a new thing; while growing up, it was forbidden because it was considered bold. She gleamed for she was beginning to realize how to express passionate feelings, but showing them to the ones she loved was hard. She didn't want rejection, so while looking in the mirror, she mustered up strength. "But I am going to learn!" With a slide of the curtain, she got in.

# 10

Jud picked up the phone. The voice he heard made his blood freeze. Instantly, he broke into a sweat. He knew that voice. It was Eurlene.

Jud reached for the back of the kitchen chair to steady himself. The chair rolled. He tried to slide, but his arms stretched until it caused him to hobble. Trying to get a better grip, he stubbed his toe on the ottoman and yelled out, "Shoot! Oh crap!" Trying to cover the mouthpiece, Jud took a tumble.

Hopping up, he was still saying oaths under his breath, trusting Karen could not hear. He could not believe what had taken place. Mr. In-Control was sprawled out on the floor with his shirt swung wide open and his bare toe throbbing. What a sight. Angrily flexing a hand into a fist and trying to keep Eurlene from guessing how this call took him off guard, he tried to gain control of his breathing, willing it to calm. Listening was a must so, very carefully, he placed the receiver to his ear and began carefully pacing the floor.

Eurlene cleared her throat. "My business partner at the bank where I work has fallen ill. The bank has asked me to step in. Out of respect only, Jud, I wanted to let you know before just showing up as the replacement of my coworker for the meeting. I'm also now the acting CPO of my bank."

Jud realized they were equals. Never in a million years did he ever think this would happen. Knowing he should say something, he fumbled for the right words. "Thanks," he finally submitted. "See you at the bank on Monday." Numb, he hung up the phone.

He knew how to handle business professionally, but this woman would open up a new can of worms. Another Pandora's box! And the march of life moved forward for Jud. Glancing at the bathroom door he thought all was well; the meeting was not until Monday so he would approach it then.

Reaching for his guitar inside the hall closet he looked over his shoulder. "Karen, come sit a spell."

"Be there in a minute. I'll get some refreshments."

She carried iced tea and finger sandwiches to the table. Taking a seat, he looked at her and began to play. Slowly at first, and then he picked up the beat.

Karen always enjoyed his strumming, but she noticed something was different. He seemed more intense than usual. She pushed her thoughts aside and felt the rhythm. She snapped her fingers and began swaying.

The doorbell rang. Jud yelled, "It's open."

Sara poked her head in. "Hi, I had some free time. Ken volunteered to take care of Timmy for a while." Karen motioned to Sara and gave the sofa a pat.

"Sit here."

Sara smiled and sat down.

Jud began a song. Karen and Sara joined in. Time passed. They sang many songs and choruses. Plenty of foot tapping and snapping of the fingers went on. Jud stopped playing. He looked at the ladies. "Let's go and get a foot-long hotdog and try it with coney sauce and sauerkraut."

Sara nodded and made a quick call to Ken, letting him know where she was going.

"What a real treat," the ladies said in unison. "We've been missing out, Jud."

The weeks passed quickly. At around midmorning, Sara called Karen. But the phone didn't ring. Puzzled, Sara said, "Hello."

"Hello?"

Sara gasped. "Karen, you surprised me."

"Why?"

"Well, the phone never rang on my end."

"Really?"

"Karen, are you free to come over? We need to go shopping."

"Come on over here about ten. Okay, Sara."

"All right."

Karen hurried with the chores, knowing Sara was excited about her and Ken's upcoming anniversary. It was in a few weeks. There was a knock at the door. Karen picked up her purse and stepped outside to join Sara.

"I wanted a new outfit from the store. Not one of my hand-made ones like I usually do."

Karen pondered on what a great seamstress Sara was and how she made most of her own clothes, and sometimes she had made her a few outfits.

"I want my new outfit to make Ken's eyes pop, and I want to surprise him and have a complete makeover from head to foot.

"Sara, you have really toned up. You look great." Jud pulled into the driveway. "Ladies, it looks like you're going shopping. I don't mind going with you. I know you want to roam from store to store." He lifted his shoulders. "I have some free time."

Karen looked at Sara and nodded. "All right, Jud, you can tag along."

He seemed amused. Jud joked a lot with the ladies.

Both shrugged, looking at one another. "Let's go."

Store after store they walked and looked. Jud pointed. "Look, there's a new woman's store. Its sign is pointing to the back in the corner nook." Happily they walked in. He motioned to Karen, showing her he found a place to sit.

Sara picked out a few outfits and went to try them on. She stepped out from the dressing room and Jud put his thumb under his lapel and roll his big green eyes.

"Sara, this is the one." Karen clasped her hands and expressed amusement at the teasing between the two of them. Karen handed Sara the selection she chose.

It was a sophisticated blend of cotton/linen fabric in a bright canary yellow. The suit was perfect for Sara. It had black piping on the lapel and weaved throughout the kick pleat. The jacket was a long squared box shape. It had scalloping around the neck. The sleeves were three-quarters in length. The sheerness of the fabric gave almost a nude look. Her skirt was a pencil fit and had a flare of pleats at the bottom. The kick pleat sat high making it really eye-catching and striking. She slid her feet into stiletto heels of black satin, which encased tiny yellow bows. They laced up the legs. Sara carried a similar purse and with gloved hands she reached for the wide-rimmed hat.

Jud unfolded himself from the chair. He had humor showing in his eyes. "Wow. Ken's in real trouble now."

Sara looked at Karen then clapped her hands. Sara seemed quite satisfied. She changed her clothes and made the purchase.,

Jud dropped Sara off at her house. Out his window, he teasingly said, "Take it easy on the old boy tonight. He has to work tomorrow!"

Sara saw him watching her out his rearview mirror. Her cheeks turned pink as she shyly said, "Jud, he'll make it to work, but don't expect too much."

The shopping and drive made Karen tired. She took Jud's hand. "Sweetie, I need a little rest, so I'm going to lie down. Give me about an hour. Okay?"

Jud gave her a pat and brought his lips to her palm. "I'll be outside if you need me."

Jud fiddled around the garage putting the mower away, hanging up the ladder and sweeping the floor. Sweat was standing on his brow as thoughts injected; meeting Eurlene after all this time, years really, unnerved him. The memories haunted him, and tons came flooding in.

He swatted at his forehead. He needed to talk with Karen about this Eurlene situation. *I'll talk with her after her rest.*

Out of nowhere came a splitting headache. Jud instantly was sick to his stomach. He had to sit down. He placed his face in his hands trying not to pass out. He felt very light headed. The pounding increased and seemed louder. He went to lie down. It was the only remedy. He needed a dark area and hot steaming towels placed over his face. He was glad the lights were off in the garage.

The sun beat through the window, using Karen to awake. She checked the clock, and an hour had passed. She entered the kitchen looking out the window and didn't see Jud. She open the garage door noticed Jud was lying on the floor. She stepped outside to get a closer look. His color seemed off somewhat and pale. She flung a hand to her mouth to keep from scream-ing. She became frightened. She had never seen Jud in a weak manner. She went and got a cold towel and placed it around his neck.

She was surprised when he jumped. He held his head.

"Karen, I didn't hear you come out." "Shush."

She began massaging his neck and back going up and down his shoulders and spine. Eventually he reached for her hands.

"What happen? Are you feeling better? You have more color in your face now."

"I've got a headache. Thanks, and yes, the pain has passed. It left me as quickly as it came."

He turned his head toward Karen, and a kiss was given. She felt his warmth against her mouth, and she responded.

He spoke tenderly. "This time I will be considerate, gentle, and patient. I only want to make you happy and totally please you." Without waiting, he swept her up.

She let a giggled slip. His arms rippled and passion passed from their eyes.

"Karen, will this hurt you or the baby? Have you talked with the doctor?"

Instead of answering, she pressed her lips on his. It seemed as if she could not get enough kisses and mingling of their tongues. He carried her ever so tenderly to their bed. Both lay silently beside each other, saying not a word. Placing one hand on the bed, his other reached touching her back. In an arch they moved closer together. Taking not a minute longer she grabbed at his lustrous hair and pulled him closer until their lips met again, slowly giving one kiss after another. Edging closer and nearer they felt heat.

Karen felt Jud rising to the mood as he slowed their pace down. He touched her shoulder and dropped kisses there while reaching for her lips, pulling and sucking on them. His hands moved automatically, sliding down her arms, one finger at a time. She shivered but reached out to him, touching, patting, and running her hands up and down his spine. She traced his belly button and reached for his jeans', button.

He groaned.

Lying on the bed Karen reached for Jud and he covered her movements and inwardly little by little she arched until they entwined, becoming complete as one.

The next morning Karen received a call from Sara.

"Hello?"

"Hi, it's me." Sara begun talking a mile a minute, and Karen could not get a word in edgewise. Karen listened. Stretching the phone cord, she poured a cup of hot brewed tea. Karen saw a note lying on the table. *I will call you later. I truly love you.*

She knew Jud had left for the office earlier. "Karen, you there?"

"I'm here."

Sara kept on talking.

Karen held the note to her breast, her heartbeat was uneven and a tear dropped. She felt reddening creep up her neck, while reading it again.

Sara seemed caught in her own world as well. Here it was in black and white written to Karen those three precious words. "I love you." Karen's heart fluttered, and her breathing became unsteady. She pinched herself, and then realized Sara had asked her a question. Karen thought it was a good thing Sara kept on talking. Karen tried to refocus using better listening skills to what her friend was saying. It sounded like she was describing her evening with Ken.

Karen interrupted. "Sara, start over from the beginning. What about your anniversary evening?"

Sara snorted. "Our date night became more interesting than planned or imagined. Ken phoned me later toward evening asking me to meet him at the restaurant. It's my favorite place. The family-owned one—Rosetta's. You know I dropped Timmy off at Mom's. Well, when I showed up, Ken was already there waiting on me. He had reserved a table and said he was glad he was sitting down when I came for he would have been on the floor the way I was looking in that sexy yellow outfit. He was shocked at the hat. He kept pointing at my head."

Sara giggled. "Karen, he looked stunned. The lights were dimmed and the candles were burning. He had flowers sitting on the table. The smell of fresh bread was everywhere. As they brought out the meal the aroma of the pasta sauce was about unbearable. It wafted through the air. I was starved. Ken loaded up on the bread and I didn't have any trouble eating my share, either. Karen, I had to unbutton the top of my skirt. I was glad for the jacket length. We ended up taking doggie bags home. It was so romantic. I can still hear the violins."

Karen tapped her fingers on the counter.

"Ken rode home with me. He had taken the bus to work that morning. I felt like a princess. He had opened and closed the car door for me. He gave me a quick little kiss and his voice turned husky when he told me again how seductive I looked."

Karen yawned.

"We paused and sat on the front porch swing. He motioned me to stay as he grabbed the guitar, and began serenading with song after song. It was so sweet. You know we've had very little quality time since Timmy has gotten older."

Karen interrupted. "Sara I need an intermission." She ran to the kitchen. "I'm back." She poured another cup of tea and sat down.

Sara continued. "He took my hand and went inside. He mentioned I was the total package. I touched his face and whispered, 'I'm yours.'"

He whispered back, "What a lucky and blessed guy I am."

Karen admired Sara's strong faith. She was educated and striking. Her midnight-black hair styled in a short crop and her outlined figure showing in her yellow suit was everything any red-blooded man needed.

"Karen, it was late, and we prepared for bed. I didn't wear the usual long granny gown but had purchased a nylon light blue baby-doll style."

Karen knew Sara had bought a special book of poems at the local book store in hopes to read to Ken before falling asleep.

"Finally, I laid the book down and walked toward the bed. Ken was stripped to the waist, hair flowing. He slipped on some oldies music, took my hand effortlessly, and began slow dancing. It had been way too long. We blended with each other. His long hair tickled her nose, but I snuggled closer. The evening was perfect. We had tender moments, touches, and his gentle ways subdued me. We engaged in the moment and became one."

Karen coughed, but she knew Sara thought nothing about talking with her about anything.

Afterward, Sara said she remembered her birth control pill. "I had forgotten to take it. The next morning, Ken had slipped out without casting a sound. What a dear he was to let me sleep in, but it would have been nice to give him a send-off gift."

Karen could hear Timmy hollering in the background. "Mommy, Mommy!"

At the same time, the doorbell rang at Karen's. Each lady hung up their phone to attend to her own lives' business.

# 11

Karen called out, "Who's there?" She was still in wonder at what Sara had said or had the conversation ended? It was the mailman.

He reached toward her with a form to sign and held a small package addressed to her. Hurriedly, she signed the slip.

After he left, she sat on the front porch and opened the package. To her astonishment, out fell the most beautiful white gold chain. Jud had not forgotten. She was elated; words could not express what this meant. The treasured thoughts were emerging. Jud had bought the chain as promised and even sent it to her.

As she stepped away, something stuck on the bottom of her shoe. Stretching down with one hand she pulled a sticky note from her pumps. Although smeared, it was at one time attached to the package she guessed, for the wording read "My soul mate."

"Ohh." Love shot straight to her heart as if it were a burning arrow. She wasted no time getting dressed and decided to surprise him at the bank. No, she wouldn't wait for a call from him; she would personally thank him. Carefully going through the closet for just the right thing to wear, she selected a colorful sun dress with red and yellow flowers draped in it. Vigilantly placing the white gold necklace with the lighthouse charm at her throat, she looked into the full-length mirror. The neckline only enhanced the beautiful charm. Grabbing her purse and a sweater she went to the corner to catch the bus. The wait seemed forever.

Stepping down from the bus, she had only a block and a few steps until arriving at the bank. Her head held high and walking in she felt a burst of pride in Jud for all his achievements. Everyone was going about their own business, so clutching the purse closer, she signed in and headed toward her husband's door. Her hand rose in a fist. She almost knocked when Ken intercepted.

"Karen," he gasped bewilderedly. "You okay?"

Nodding, he placed a hand on her shoulder. "Jud is still with the morning client. I only just stepped out from the room to make some copies for them. It may take another hour or two. Do you want to wait?"

Karen disappointedly shook her head. "No." Feeling instantly sad and not wanting Ken to see any tears, she turned, leaving the bank. She was so frustrated about not calling ahead first. She felt dejected.

On the way back to the bus stop, she looked across the street and spotted Jud's car. Feeling the need to rest, she went and tried the door handle. It was unlocked, so she slid into the front seat and closed the door. She was glad the windows were rolled down. Shutting her eyes, sleep came quickly. Upon waking she had become very thirsty. Knowing there was a water fountain on the corner she decided to get a drink before heading home.

It was midafternoon, and it was extremely hot outside. Cupping her hands, she remembered how Kate had shown her as a child to get a drink, which brought a little humor to mind. The fountain water was refreshing; it always kept the water cool. She didn't know how, it just did.

As Karen looked up, there was Jud. He was headed across the street toward the car. She tried to flag him with a white hanky, but a dump truck passed in front of them. The noise from the street was too loud as she called out to him. She went to step down at the curb, but by the time the light turned, Karen was swallowing the cool water. She saw he had opened the passenger's door, which seated a striking red-headed woman.

Karen wanted to scream. How could she have been so dumb? Then came a sudden realization. "I left my purse in the car! Now how am I going to get home?" She studied her options: (a) she could either go back inside the bank and ask Ken for bus fare or (b) walk. Being too embarrassed, b was the option; there was not an alternative. Being a sunny day and not wanting to confront Ken, she decided to walk. You know, a girl has her pride. Every once in a while she felt a breeze, which was a welcoming touch. She hummed and sang all the way home.

Opening the door, she was glad a kitchen chair was close by. Her feet hurt and were swollen. Sitting, she placed her feet on one of the other chairs. Then the baby moved. It felt like it was beating on a drum. She began thinking on the due date. How long did she have before the birth? She thought the baby was not due for about another two and a half months. Taking note, she would ask the doctor on the next visit. Sitting was not comfortable, but still, Karen dozed off.

Cramped in the legs and numb in the toes, she awoke to another big movement from the baby. It was hard to stand. Holding onto the counter top, her heart skipped a beat for joy, thinking they would soon be a family of three. A striking hunger had set in, and she realized she had not eaten. The idea of chicken noodle soup with crackers and a pot of freshly brewed tea sounded great. Keeping her sea legs from shaking and her blood circulating was another thing though. Karen carefully moved around the kitchen. Just getting a pan off the shelf became a chore. It was hard to reach down for her tummy got in the way. The soup seemed to hit the spot and so did the tea. After eating and tidying up she went to turn on the television.

It was on the weekend and flipping through the channels she noticed the clock on the wall read seven. She glanced out the living room window and saw that the sun was setting. She heard music and decided to watch the last part of Laurence Welk.

Time has seemed to pass by from morning so quickly. Karen had become very relaxed and determined to get ready for bed.

She moved unhurriedly, being tired and very pregnant. The bed felt great, just hard enough to be comfortable. She read a little, having a brief devotional, then turned and switched off the light. While moving into the covers, she smelled the scented pillow where Jud had lain. *Wonder where he is*, she thought as sleep took over.

The phone was ringing, and Karen fumbled to answer. "Hello, hello," she said, before she realized she was holding the phone receiver upside down.

She could hear a voice, so upon turning the receiver right side up, she said, "It's me. Hello, Jud, is it you?" The communication was bad and heavily broken. There was trouble on the line. She knew squirrels had eaten through the lines before and now it seemed like it had happened again. Karen strained to hear. All she heard him say was, "I will be gone three to five days." His voice was in a whisper. "It's a planned business trip. Sorry I didn't get to mention this to you."

"Jud, you there?"

"I love you." There was complete silence and then a terrible static noise. Karen looked at the phone and replaced the receiver to her ear. The phone cracked then went dead.

Turning on the soft light by the bed, she held the phone in hand, looking at it and felt her temperature rise. She smacked the receiver. She hadn't even been able to say anything. Not "be careful" or "call me back." She didn't even mention to him that her purse was in the backseat of the car. Now she would have to wait until he called again, if he even did. Flustered, she kept hitting the covers until she could pound no more.

Karen noticed hunger had set in once again, so she fixed peanut butter and jelly finger sandwiches. "Yum" was the only thing her mind said. The baby kicked lightly and smiling, Karen mused, while patting her belly. "So you like peanut butter and jelly too." A drink of iced tea went down really well and was refreshing.

She padded off to bed for more sleep. As a matter of fact, her whole body was weary, but sleep was elusive. She gazed at the ceiling and lay wide awake. Karen tried lying on her side but found it impossible. She had become so uncomfortable. The pillows were fluffed, and she had sat up in bed once again, switched on the light to read, and finally whispered a prayer. *I'm here. Help me.*

She was not feeling the help needed at the moment for thoughts of the redhead kept popping in her mind. Totally exhausted, Karen fell fast asleep. Karen was awakened by a pounding noise. She reached for a pillow and placed it over her head, wanting to muffle out the sounds, but it intensified.

"All right, all right, I'm coming." She scouted and found a robe and went cautiously to the door. It was her mom and dad. Karen looked puzzled, smiled, and hugged them both.

Kate put on a pot of coffee. Her dad got busy using the phone. Kate told Karen, "I came to town to meet up with Timmy's grandma, Louise. We have a project to complete. It sure is great to see you. My, the baby has grown."

Karen had questions for Kate but she knew better than to ask.

Kate searching Karen's face, said, "Your father needs to meet Nathan."

Karen's spirits lifted. "Dad, can I tag along with you?"

He had always made her feel special. Pulling her nose, he nodded.

There was never a doubt of her parents' love. She loved them in return unconditionally. Karen grabbed a slice of toast, hurriedly got dressed, and pulled on a loose, sleeveless dress Kate had made and sent her.

Nathan was pacing back and forth in the driveway when they got there. Donald hurried up the steps and both men went inside. Donald turned to Karen. "We need to do some measuring of the windows."

Karen nodded and quietly slipped down the steep basement stairway, picking up the same pillow left there from before. Angling into position, she sat down on it. She planned on cleaning the viewing glass lodged in the center of the big drain plug. But it was so full of cement dust and gunk settlements even she could not loosen or move any compound. She only made matters worst by smearing the dust. The top viewing glass had just seemed to spread and harden even more. Again she could not get a glimpse nor see anything in it at all. Raising her fist in the air, she shook it. *I will reveal the secret. Next time I'll come prepared.*

Just then her father poked his head from the top of the stairs and in his soft voice called out to her, "I'm leaving. Come on, Karen. It's time for us to go."

She paused as she ascended up the stairs, huffing and puffing like a freight train. A thought was still on her mind. *Your secret old drain plug may be safe for now, but a day is coming and it won't be.*

Donald stopped at the Coney Shop. They placed an order while Donald made several phone calls from the pay phone. When the order came, Donald went to wave his on, but Karen retrieved his arm, making the waitress sit the Coney's in front of them. Being hungry, Karen was on her third one as Donald concluded the arrangements for a car rental. He needed to use one while in town instead of a borrowed one. The other phone call made was to rent a cottage. "All the rental cottages were being remodeled and I needed to look elsewhere."

Karen jumped at the chance her folks might consider staying with her. "Jud is out of town over the next few days, and there would be enough room if you and Mom want to stay."

Donald eyebrows shot up. "He's out of town? On business?"

She tried to sound nonchalant. "Yes. He had a meeting or something."

Donald smiled as he patted his daughter's hand. "Karen, it would be nice for a stay. Your mother and I can do some catching up with you."

She clapped her hands. "Great, then it's settled. You'll stay."

The appointment with Louise took less time than Kate anticipated. Checking Karen's cupboard she saw the supplies was ample and begun dinner.

Entering the doorway Karen and Donald barked. "What smells so good?"

Kate viewed them enjoying each others company. She smiled while drying her hands. "Wash up, you two, and help set the table."

The dishes really didn't match, but the table napkins and place settings made it came together. Donald placed the last goblet of water in front of his knife. Kate served the fried chicken, garlic mashed potatoes with gravy, and green beans garnished with bacon bits while Karen carried in a large bowl of fresh garden salad. The dinner was an attractive sight. Sitting down to a home-cooked meal was wonderful.

Karen looked at her mom. "It's been a long time since eating your cooking, Mom." Karen frowned. "Jud will hate missing your home cooking."

In absolute quietness, they worked together cleaning up after the evening meal. Only a few leftovers were placed in the refrigerator. Kate knew they would be gone before the evening was over; either her husband or Karen would later indulge. With the kitchen swept and the trash emptied they all proceeded to the living room. They sat one on the sofa and Karen sat in the comfortable recliner. They conversed with one another late into the evening.

Kate brought in some sweet rolls with a fresh pot of brewed tea and a new cup of black coffee for Donald. It had been nice to enjoy their time together visiting with each other.

Karen stood. "I'll get the bed blankets and sheets down to make the up the sofa bed for you." Karen half-smiled. "I'm going to turn in." As she waddled to bed, she heard her folks say, "Good night."

Lying there, she sent a prayer upward. *Watch over him, please.*

Karen spirits plummeted, and a case of blues settled in. She missed Jud not being there. She pounded the pillow, but still, there was not the closeness or him or the sweet nothings in her ear. Karen felt abandoned. She knew her parents were in the other room talking, but it was all a big buzz.

She took a book and began to read. Chapter 1.

*He rode off in the horizon.* Tears came.

Karen needed to use the bathroom, and she washed her face. Drained, she fell into a deep sleep, but her mind kept working. The same recurring dream came. It was about Eurlene's being with Jud. It continuing until it became a bad nightmare. Karen would be replaced by the redhead in scenes with Jud. The kiss was to encompass Karen, but it would switch to it being the redhead's face instead. Sleep came, but rest was not there. She felt more exhausted than ever. She awoke in a fog and gave a huge sigh.

The phone rang, or had she been dreaming? No, it was definitely the phone. Grabbing her robe, she headed toward the kitchen to answer. On the way, she caught the hem on the rocker. It made a clunking noise. She pulled the bottom flap; it loosened. She was breathing heavily as she went to answer the phone.

"Hello." The only sound she heard was the dial tone. Sitting down, tears fell from the red-rimmed eyes. She held her arms and rocked back and forth while having a pity party.

All the lights went on; both of her parents had jumped up. Her mother handed her a cup of hot tea, adding one lump of sugar. Kate placed a hand on her daughter's shoulder and patted it.

Donald dressed, and went back to eating. He gave his mouth a wipe, pinched Kate and gave her a quick squeeze, and left. Kate likewise had gotten dressed. She reached for her hat and purse and went out the door. Looking over her shoulder, "I'll be with Florence for the day."

Karen had heard Florence pull up and beep the horn. She picked the chore of washing their clothes. She hoped Jud would call instead.

Sara and Ken pulled in front of Karen's place. He grabbed Timmy's toy bag and walked with Sara to the door.

Karen was on the porch waiting. "Hi, Timmy, Sara, and Ken." She gave them hugs.

"Ladies, I'll be back late to pick up Sara and Timmy."

Sara pulled Ken's long, straight, black pony tail. He stopped, gave a little peck and swung her around. Timmy squealed and began to cry when Ken left.

Sara said, "We need to have a girls' talk with my best friend, and here's hoping Timmy would let us."

Karen fed him a warm bottle of milk while rocking him, and it settled Timmy right down. Sara lifted and laid him on the sofa for a two-hour nap. He rolled over clutching a stuff toy and was soon out like a light.

Sitting and talking was like old times. Sara laughed and recalled again how she looked in the yellow suit with the tiny bows on her shoes they had picked out. Sara showed Karen a picture of Ken and her.

Karen raved. "You two looked so cute."

Sara blushed. "The owners of the restaurant took it before we left."

Karen pulled her necklace out from her blouse and showed Sara the white gold chain. "Jud got it for me. It's a herringbone."

Sara noticed the little lighthouse charm Karen had placed on it. Both Karen and Sara laughed. "Remember our 'penny swear necklaces.'"

"Did you put yours in the handmade memory box we made? I did!"

"Yes, me too."

Sara looked seriously at Karen. "Can you talk about your getaway? Boy, was I surprised when you two left."

"Well, Jud relaxed and planned a nice surprise picnic. He also played the guitar. Of course, the ladies stopped and swooned. He played into them." Karen gave off a silly giggle and then blushed. "Sara, Jud said he loves me."

Sara realized she had been holding her breath and let out a long sigh. She experienced instant relief. "Maybe there will be no divorce? It sounded like a fairy tale, Karen."

Timmy let out a yelp. Sara went running.

The kitchen door banged. "Yoohoo." Kate came in carrying two long banana boxes and set them down against the outside wall. Donald followed right behind. "Kate, I am starved." Then seeming to notice company, he croaked, "Hi, Sara. It sure is nice to see you and Timmy." He ruffled Timmy's hair. "Hi, little man."

Of course, the phone began ringing. Karen could not get up quick enough, and Donald reached for the phone. When he was finished talking, he placed the phone on the receiver.

Ken had also slipped in the back door. "You didn't give up on me, did you?"

She watched Karen shake her head. It felt like Grand Central Station.

Kate was puttering around the kitchen when Donald suggested, "Kate, why not order in?"

She paused only for a moment and smiled. "Okay."

Donald had Kate ordered for everyone. It was a surprised when the chicken in the basket arrived shortly.

"What a great and unexpected treat," Karen mused.

He stole the show. In one hand, Timmy was so adorable while holding onto a blanket. With the other, he reached for anything at his height and brought it down to the floor. Everyone took their turn with him. He was held and kissed by everyone. The funny part was when Ken convinced Timmy to play horsy. It took forever for him to straddle his dad's back. Everyone laughed and laughed. Timmy would squeal. "More, Daddy. Giddy up."

Ken called Timmy "Sport," and sometimes he would answer to it. "Just one more time around the room and we'll call its quits." Ken's hair came out of the pony tail, so he removed the band, allowing it to flow freely.

Eyes were on them both. Ken's skinny legs really showed in his cargo shorts. He did look spruce up in his casual clothes, and it was nice to see him without a suit and tie for a change.

Timmy continued playing on the floor with the new dump truck Ken had bought while the adults ate the food. Ken soon placed Timmy in a seat, pulling him up to the table and sitting him at eye level, and helped Timmy to eat.

With Timmy in hand, Sara and Ken bid their good-bye as they left for home.

Karen struggled but took out the trash after partly straightening up the kitchen. Standing in the garage only reminded her of Jud. *Wonder what he's doing?*

# 12

Dawn came, and it showed a sunny day. Kate picked up the boxes from the kitchen and placed them into the rental car. She gave Donald a kiss and waved to Karen as she drove off and went about her business.

Patting the sofa, Donald motioned for Karen to come sit with him. She welcomed their treasured time together. Flipping through the channels, they watched television for the morning news. There were three things Donald always did: (1) read devotions, (2) read the paper, and (3) listen to or watch the news report when he could.

Karen carefully placed her feet upon the coffee table. She scooted around, trying to get comfortable. The baby started kicking. She thought the outline of the baby could be traced. She looked over at her dad, and all she could do was smile. News was over, and her father muted the TV. "I want you to know Jud called earlier."

Karen set up. "I missed him again?"

Donald stood. "Jud was just checking in. He wanted to make sure everything was all right. He wanted me to tell you he missed and loved you." With raised eyebrows, he looked at Karen. "Eurlene, a client, is with him and he mentioned she is a cracker."

Karen nodded then dropped her smile. She scrunched her face and felt somewhat light-headed. Unfolding from the chair, she wondered if the redhead was Eurlene. The last image she had was a woman getting onto her husband's car. She had curly, bouncy, fiery-red hair, and was in an all-too-short-fitting suit, wearing six- to nine-inch heels.

When Kate returned, Karen did the honors pouring some hot tea. Donald shut off the television. "Kate, lead us in some singing."

Kate quirked her body but soon led them in a song. They did some singing but knew it really wasn't Donald's forte. They each enjoyed having good, quality family time of being together.

Karen had settled down, but the baby hadn't. "Mom, Dad, I think the baby is swimming." They laughed.

Karen realized while yawning how tiredness had set in. "I'm going to try and lay down."

They waved her on. "Sweet dreams." Kate blew her a kiss.

She was grateful to climb into bed. First she tried propping up her feet for again there were problems. Her feet were swelling a lot. It became another one of those sleepless afternoons with rushing thoughts. Who was the redhead and why was she with her hus-band? Why had her purse not been mentioned?

Karen could not get comfortable in any position. There was not any arrangement to be found, not even in sitting or laying down for any length of time. Her stomach had been pushed out to the limit. The baby seemed to have grown a lot in the past two weeks. Nothing seemed to help. She tried using pillows to elevate her feet. There just was not any relief; her feet pained her most of the time.

She thought she would be better if only she could hear Jud's voice. She needed his arms to feel comfort and be assured. Darkness drifted in, and sleep came.

Karen had not had a conversation with Jud to let him know anything about attending the hair styling program. Donald stay at the house in case Jud called. They did not want him to worry unnecessarily about Karen and the baby.

Her mother postponed their leave date so she could attend the style show with her daughter. It meant everything for Karen to keep her cosmetology licenses she had worked so hard to obtain. It had taken two years of school, plus the board testing. Kate drove because Karen was too huge to fit behind the steering wheel and she felt miserable.

Karen sighed. "It's a poor time to be made to attend this show."

Kate just grunted.

The baby kept pushing, causing Karen to feel so much pressure it seemed like peeing became routine every half hour.

"It looked like the baby has dropped into a lower position," Karen told her mom.

Kate took a quick glance, and at the red light, she placed her hand on Karen's stomach. "It's not too far off."

After the intense four-hour show and drilling questions, and with certificate in hand, Karen and Kate left. It was going to be a long drive home. They stopped only to use the bathroom and, of course, get fries for Karen. Kate ordered a large black coffee to drink on the remainder of the trip. The trip was so exhausting for both of them.

Early the next morning, Kate appeared with puffy eyes.

"You all right, Mom?"

I'm a little tired Karen, but I'll sleep on the plane." She gave Karen a brief hug as she turned to Donald.

"Where's your list of calls?"

Karen enjoyed watching how they worked together.

"All that's left is going to the airport, dropping off the rental car, checking in our luggage, and catching our flight." With suitcases in hand each of her parents said their good-byes. "We promise to keep in touch."

Karen knew their trip had been planned for over a month. She noticed they were so excited to be off on another one of their adventures.

The phone rang. Karen hoped it was Jud. "Hello."

"Karen, you'll never believe this." It was her mother's voice coming across the line. "We stepped in line to board our flight, but we were stopped. The flight attendant warned us there was an hour delay because of rain."

Her mom gave a slight laugh. "Your dad and I are going to buy some magazines while waiting. I didn't want you to worry if we were late calling you. Take care of yourself. We love you."

Karen continued to be exhausted and miserable. The pressure kept mounting up. Karen had a doctor's appointment on Tuesday and was glad Sara was tagging along. The baby moved so much Karen had black and blue marks located on each of her rib sides. She didn't know what the doctor would think about the bruises.

Tuesday arrived, and there was not a cloud in the sky. Karen had Sara meet her at the bus stop. The ladies were traveling to the doctor's office, but on the way there, the bus broke down. They had to get off the bus and stand at the designated stop and wait for another bus to haul them to the doctor's office, which was located on a busy street three miles further. There wasn't a seat left, so they stood. Karen whimpered to Sara, "My legs look out of place, and my feet are so swollen my shoes really hurt."

Sara gave a quizzed smile. She tucked Karen's arm in hers. "I found out the bus we were riding had a flat tire, and of course, it was on the side we were sitting. No wonder it was almost impossible for you to get up."

Karen hunched her shoulders as the new bus appeared. They boarded, and it rattled and shook all the way there. It was almost too much for Karen to handle.

Getting off, Sara said, "The office is only a couple of blocks to walk."

Each step Karen felt to her like her last. She stepped the right foot in front, and the left one wouldn't move. Karen felt a stab of pain pushing upward in her back. "Sara, help me."

Sara got behind her and lifted Karen's left foot. She held her hand and tried to give friendly support. Finally the door opened at the doctor's office. The little bell hanging there greeted each person coming and going.

The nurse addressed Karen as they came through the door. "You just missed the doctor. I am sorry. He was called away on another emergency."

Going to the scheduling book, the nurse seemed to notice her condition. "We will call you for the next appointment and make sure he's here. Now, if you have any doubts or questions, don't hesitate; go straight into the hospital."

Karen began crying. Tears were rolling down her face. The hormones made her feel dejected. Karen could go no further at the moment and just sat down. Sara handed her a tissue and gently rubbed her back.

"It will be all right. This far along into the pregnancy, it is hard, but it will pass. Come on, Karen." Karen nudged Sara. Sliding a prayer upward, she said, "See your humble servants?"

After Karen pulled herself together, they braved the return walk to the bus stop and rode the bus one more time. They proceeded on the bus back to Karen's house. This time there was not any kind of trouble. Karen and Sara were relieved.

Karen cried without a sound from her discomfort and awkwardness.

While the Camilla tea brewed, Sara made some peanut butter and jelly sandwiches for them to eat along with homemade, leftover chicken noodle soup. They ate, and Sara poured them each a cup of tea. Sara eventually helped Karen to bed. Karen motioned to her puffy feet. "They look like water balloons."

Sara pried off her shoes and lifted her legs, placing Karen's feet upon two pillows.

"Try and rest, friend. Keep those sore feet up and let the swelling reduce."

Karen just wanted to sleep. She was drifting when she heard Sara close the door. She knew Sara would be walking home. Karen did not try to put up a fuss, for the act of lying down seemed wonderful. She knew some rest was much needed.

Her legs and feet were swollen. The skin looked paper-thin. She tried to touch them, but only white marks showed. It hurt to touch. Karen reelevated her feet higher than her heart, trying to release the pressure and tightness she felt. Karen felt she looked like a Goodyear Blimp.

The next few days, Karen did only what had to be done and absolutely nothing more. She thought if a pin pricked her skin, she would burst.

Sara called. "How are you doing? Are you resting?" Karen snorted after Sara's fifth call. "I'm miserable. Go away."

Ken had picked up a few groceries and a couple of magazines for Karen at her request. She wanted some new reading material. Ken would ring the bell, place his bike against the porch and wait on Karen to come out. If he used his car it would be left running, for he never went inside Karen's house alone. Karen appreciated he was a very careful man and that he cared about his and her reputation. Karen felt eyes were always on her. Karen joked with Sara once, calling him a "one-woman man."

"He better be." Sara had laughed in return. Karen admired Ken. "I truly trusted him." Karen put together a few snacks of celery and pretzels smothered in peanut butter. She couldn't get enough. She was really enjoying the peanut butter when the phone rang. Getting up was another matter; it became so hard. She would lift herself up, and then stabilized her legs. Her feet seemed like a mile apart. She could not hurry and toddled as she picked up the phone. "Hello."

Her doctor's nurse was at the other end. "I made an appointment for you this Friday morning at ten. Is that okay?"

Letting out a long breath, she was both glad and sad. "Yes that's fine. I'll be there." She reached for pen and paper and jotted down the date and time.

She, beyond a doubt, wanted to know the progress of the baby, but going there to his office would be another grave ordeal. She called Sara. "Hi. It's the blimp. Can you go with me to the doctor's office Friday morning? It's at ten."

"Sure. We need to know when the baby is due." "You can?" Karen let out another sigh. "Oh, good." She smacked some more of the peanut butter onto a spoon and yawned.

Karen finally fell asleep. Karen woke up suddenly when a beam of light sifted through the window. There was Jud-lying in the recliner. Her heart gave a wave. Sitting up in bed, she rubbed her eyes while peeking through the door and saw he had not shaven. She could see his loose tie and a now-wrinkled jacket. She smiled. He remembered to lay it across the arm. It must have been right before dozing off.

Why was he still in suit clothes? They looked crumpled. She knew it was so unlike him. She had to make sure she was not dreaming, so she edged very carefully from the bed and slowly toddled into their living room.

Suddenly she saw movement on the couch and screamed. Jud immediately jumped up and came running. Again she yelled. Karen shakily turned on a light and there was the red-headed woman sitting on their green sofa.

"What are you doing in my house?" Karen instantly had to sit down and looking up, she saw Tom holding a cup of tea for her. "Breakfast anyone?"

Karen thought for a moment. *Yes, this was another bad dream.* She pinched herself and then knew it was not a dream but was real.

Tom kissed Karen on the cheek again. "Come and get it."

Karen, with a questioning expression, took only a piece of toast. Her stomach was cramping. Tom's soft voice and beckoning eyes assured her all this would be explained and all soon would pass. He looked so trusting. Jud took a mug of black coffee and handed the red-headed woman one.

Karen's tea was refreshed by Jud with a strained smile. As Jud went to kiss Karen, she moved her head. He knew her eyes were telling a story all their own. Karen hit the pillow on her lap and bit her lip. "Jud you had no right bringing her here. This is my house." Karen's eyes had darken and specks like darts seemed to flash, but Jud appeared clueless.

Tom placed a hand on Karen's shoulders and offered her a feeble beckoning smile. "Now, Karen, let me explain. Eurlene, this is Karen, Jud's wife."

With corners of his mouth turned up, Jud squatted next to Karen, glancing back and forth from his dad to the ladies.

"Karen, this Eurlene." He quickly went to the kitchen adding, "Eurlene was promoted to a new position from her bank, and she now carries an equal title as Jud."

Karen's eyes widened. Her only reply slipped out. "Oh?"

Tom continued. "Jud's position held at the bank allowed him to deal only with this occasion or equal chair. Eurlene became a business client and nothing more. Her bank preferred Eurlene to conduct bank business only with Jud's." Tom took Karen's cup, focused with a sweet smile, and quickly announced, "I joined Jud on this trip also."

He again strolled into the kitchen, setting down her cup.

Karen kept looking at Eurlene. She was downright staring at her. She remembered this was the redhead. Jud had confided the information about her before they were married. Tapping her now fat fingers on the arm of the chair, she spoke through gritted teeth. "So, this is Eurlene in the flesh after all these years." In her mind, she was screaming. *His ex-girlfriend, you know, the one who did not keep the baby.* But Karen knew how to be proper no matter what, so she mentioned nothing. She plastered a meager smile on her lips. Karen struggled, but she rose to her feet. Her stomach began churning; sickness had settled in. Waddling from the room, arms at her sides, she barked, "I need to get some fresh air. Tom, please hand me out a cup of ice."

Jud had been correct in his mental detail about her facial expressions. He knew Karen was going to be a force to reckon with.

He watched Karen make a trip back inside to use the restroom. He was convinced she stayed in there longer than usual. He knocked on the door. "You okay?"

The door opened. She was narrow-eyed. Jud looked perplexed as she passed him prudishly in the hall. He saw that Karen had changed clothes. Their shoulders touched. A flare signal was sent to his mind as if he had been burned.

Jud, being drained, excused himself by closing the bathroom's door. He stepped into the shower and felt the hot water cascade over his head and then his shoulders. He was glad to feel relief even if it was brief. After shaving, he got dressed in another light blue shirt and dress slacks. He had folded the sleeves up on the shirt like always.

Jud glanced outside and saw Karen. He watched as she opened the car door. Karen was retrieving something. Curiosity made him trek outside. "Karen what are you doing?"

Karen snorted. She turned and began to slip. Her house shoe came off.

Jud rushed to her side trying to steady her. "Hold on to me." He placed one hand on her elbow as he braced against her and slipped the fluffy slipper on her foot.

He thought. *I know the idea to explain the trip situ-ation to Karen should have been done before bringing Eurlene to our home. But now it is too late!*

Karen twitched and pinched Jud's forearm. Looking at her he saw pain. She had placed her hands on his back.

"What is it, Karen?" he asked barely above a whisper.

She let out a long sigh. "Pain is shooting through my lower back." She gasped as tears streamed down her cheek.

Her cry clenched his gut. He knew by the sound she was in trouble and needed to be at the hospital. She had gotten much bigger in the last few days than he remembered. Karen still had on the necklace he had purchased at the camp. He became full of hope. He ran his fingers through his hair and looked over at Tom without saying a word.

Tom took charge. "Jud, take Karen. I will follow you to the hospital."

Jud glanced over his shoulder at Eurlene. She waved. "Be on your way. I'm a big girl."

Tom had made most of the necessary phone calls before leaving. First he called Ken. "Will you call Karen's parents and let them know Jud is taking Karen to the hospital? Some sort of back pain."

Ken replied, "Sure, I will call them. Anything else?"

"Not right now. Well, maybe a prayer or two wouldn't hurt." He hung up the phone.

# 13

Turning, Tom saw Jud pacing. He tapped him on the shoulder. "Jud, why are you waiting? Now get. Take Karen and go to the hospital." Tom asked Eurlene, "Do you want to stay here or ride with me to the hospital?"

She grabbed her purse. "Let's go. Want me to drive?"

Silently Tom shook his head. He quickly gathered his things and they slipped into Jud's car. They followed the ambulance there.

Ken and Sara soon arrived at the hospital after arrangements had been made with Timmy's grandma. Ken had known Eurlene from their meeting at the bank, plus Jud had confided about their past. Ken could not help gazing at her. He had to admit she was a looker, slender but curvy, a very handsome woman. Ken could not help noticing all the men stopping or turning their heads just trying to get a glimpse of her.

He watched as she batted and fluttered her eyes. He had to admit Eurlene defiantly knew how to get attention. It seemed she demand the stares of people. In a crazy way, she controlled the atmosphere about her.

Sara stepped on Ken's foot, bringing him back to reality. He shrugged, flouncing a humble smile. He gave Sara a big hug and grabbed her hand.

Jud was in the hospital's billing office, signing a new group of papers for the admission of Karen. He finally finished the completed paperwork and was set on his way to her.

Jud, seeing the chapel sign, stopped off for a quick moment; he wanted to try to collect his thoughts. He had just sat down when he felt a hand resting on his back. Jud did not realize tears were staining his face until he felt a drop hit his hand. As he turned and looked over his shoulder there stood Eurlene. She gracefully moved between the pews and set next to him.

Casually she placed a hand on his knee. "Jud, I now know this Comforter, also. He really listens." Then she sat there in silence for the longest time. Their upward thoughts were on Karen and the safety of the baby.

Jud heard steps. Ken had caught up to them. "Jud step into the hall. I have a cup of joe. It's strong and black."

Wringing his hands, Jud stood. "Thanks, Ken." Being composed once again, Jud walked tall and placed a makeshift smile on his face, checking his charm to be intact. Jud looked into the mirror hanging on the wall and noticed the hollowness in his face. Imperceptible lines had appeared, and it must have been from the lack of much-needed sleep and also the issues lying silent between him and Karen. The lack of eye expression told it all.

As he headed toward her room, he checked the unsaid memory and forced a smile as he sauntered into the room. "Karen, how beautiful you look. You are all geared up."

"The doctor ordered more blood work. Five tubes to be exact." She crunched up her little nose and Jud broke out into laughter. Jud thought how wonderful yet sad it was to see Karen. "I did not mean for you to be startled with Eurlene, Tom, or even myself in coming home. I should have called you, but the phones played static every time we tried. I am so sorry for not trying again." He hung his head. "Karen, I feel horrible. Did this possibly cause you this trip to the hospital?"

He took her hand but couldn't control the shake. He looked into her eyes pleading, but he could tell Karen was still angry. He bit his lip to keep quiet and squeezed her small hand.

Jud had heard a helicopter and knew Karen's parents had arrived. He also knew they were with Sara, Tom, and Ken. Jud rounded his shoulders. They were all waiting to hear an update about Karen. No one had said what took place or knew why she had been admitted to the hospital. He thought Tom, Ken, and Eurlene may have an idea, but didn't venture to talk.

At last Jud strolled over to the men and quietly spoke. "The only news is, Karen was resting." He explained. "The doctor said Karen is much larger than he had expected at this time in her pregnancy. He is also concerned with the amount of water she is holding."

He shook his head. "She seems in so much pain. Her feet and hands are badly swollen, and it's from the pressure of the baby. The doctor insisted the baby is right on schedule and due in about a week, maximum two, although the doctor didn't rule out with the first it could be late or early.

Tom let Jud know he had already introduced Eurlene to Karen's parents as a new business client of his. He continued, "They have a few business forms that need to be signed and legalized quickly."

Jud found Kate glaring at Eurlene. He watched Kate move closer to Sara and heard her request. "Assist me as I walk." They stopped and stood just a little distance across the hall from the men. Moving from one foot to the other, Kate nodded at Sara and while covering her mouth. "She's some looker."

But Jud could hear.

Sara stayed next to Ken and kept a closed month.

Jud beaded his eyes on both ladies. "Karen really needs everyone to band together and be strong at a time such as this."

Jud, still very concerned about their unfinished business, had taken a stretching break and walked. He needed to get the left-behind brief case from the car. The contracts needed to be complete with Eurlene's signature and Jud as witness, and also set before the attorney. He wanted to get everything wrapped up; the window of time was closing in. He just wanted the assignment with Eurlene to be finished and things turned back to normal. He wanted Eurlene gone. As much as he enjoyed gaining the business and her business sense, the time had come for her to return and be on her merry way.

Jud's father had questions. Jud lifted his hand and motioned a time out. "Looking at Eurlene, you notice she is like a fine piece of art. But I don't intend adding her to my collection. Dad, I moved in her direction once a long time ago. Now it is only business. She is not what I need. Karen is." Sitting at the hospital café taking a sip of coffee, he looked at his dad. "Eurlene would make a beautiful trophy on someone's arm. I only wish her the best out of life, but honestly, not with me."

Tom sat down his cup and patted Jud on the shoulder. "I understand. I'm glad you find no interest in anyone except your wife, Karen."

"Dad, I love her. She's my life. I only hope it's not too late." Turning on his heel, he darted back into Karen's room and found she was still being monitored and was unwavering for the time being. Gently lifting her head, he placed a soft fluffy pillow under it. Karen appeared to have fallen into a deep sleep. He blew a kiss down to her and in silence left the room.

Jud then faced questions from Karen's parents about the fiery redhead. "Jud, what is she doing with you here at the hospital?"

Tom stepped over to the family and overrode Jud's speaking. "Donald, Kate, it's a business deal. We needed Spencer and the work had to be finished here."

Donald raised his hand in skepticism, but Kate shushed him.

The family rallied in assurance Karen's hospital trip certainly was not his fault. Donald even embraced Jud. "It comes with being pregnant."

Kate agreed. "She's in a good place." She prattled on. "Boy, that was some trip we made for Karen to continue her cut-and-color license. She needs a rest. I sure did."

Jud raised his eyebrows. Tom walked over and nudged Jud. "Let's conclude all this bank business with Eurlene tonight?"

Kate touched Jud's arm. "I'll stay with Karen. You get this settled!"

Tom explained to Donald, "You know they need to leave here and finish the unsigned papers. If everyone in agreement tonight we can get them notarized."

Donald shook his head. "Wait for me; I'm going too." Sounding like a bear, he said, "I'll be a witness."

The four men and shapely Eurlene left the hospital. They crowded into the back seat leaving Jud to drive with Eurlene up front. Upon arriving at the bank Jud had made arrangements for Eurlene and the attorney Spencer to meet. In business mode, Jud had all the papers already drawn up. She just needed to sign the contract. It needed to be witnessed and copied.

The attorney sat briefcase down. He spread the necessary papers on the desk and placed his seal work to the side. Eurlene fluttered her eyes, signed, and shook the men's hand. Spencer made a pounding noise giving his stamp of approval on the contract. Jud waited for Spencer to finish and walked him out the door. Outside, Spencer stopped. "Jud, I hope fate is good to me again." A smirk came across Spencer's face.

Jud's eyebrows knitted in puzzlement, and cocking his head, he listened.

Tapping his briefcase, Spencer caught Jud's eye. "When the time is right, maybe Eurlene and I will meet again."

Jud, being amused, gave a hardy pat on his back and in unheard tones went on hypothetically, "Give her a call sometime if you are up to the challenge."

Walking toward the car, Tom assured Donald, "Jud still wants to honor his marriage with Karen because he truly loves her. Even though he senses Karen at this time does not love him in return. He knows there something even if it is a great respect."

"But why did he see Spencer before?"

"Donald, he saw the attorney to inform him about his week-end getaway with Karen, and how it changed his mind about everything." Tom smiled while slapping him on the back. "The information our children shared gave Jud enough hope they may have a workable future together."

Jud had been standing a few cars away, but voices had carried so he listened. At their silence Jud ambled and joined his father and Donald. "Everything all right?"

Tom placing his hand on Jud's back. "It's going to be."

Donald broke in, eyes looking at Tom then at Jud. "Tom, you already know this, but Jud, you need to take heed in what I say."

Jud looked puzzled at both men. He opened his car door. "Shall we get in?"

Before pulling away, Donald placed a gripped hand on Jud's shoulder. "Listen to me."

Jud saw deep concern from his father-in-law. With a start, Jud unfolded himself from his seat. He took a deep breath. The air seemed fresher. Gathering his thoughts he couldn't quite shake Donald's grip, or his stern narrow eyes.

Jud could feel Donald's stare and he took a step backward, spread his legs, and braced his fists at sides. "What?"

Donald also stepped backward and touched Jud's arm. "Don't be so willful. People always need to share or be willing to communicate with one another. If you want to succeed you don't have secrets or hide them from each other."

Jud frowned.

Donald shook Jud's arm softly. "That will stifle any friendships, and especially marriage. There is nothing to build on and it will not last. It can only crumble. Honestly, it's doomed before it even begins."

Jud shuffled his feet but never lost eye contact with Donald.

"Son, whether in the good times or in the valleys, you always, but always need to converse. Commit yourself and communicate. Won't you try with Karen?"

Jud fumbled for the right words, moving his foot in the gravel. "We've begun."

"I strongly suggest you take the vows of this marriage seriously!"

Jud flinched, nodded, and took another step backward. He felt struck, but he knew he had heard only the truth. Looking upward, he sensed God's presence. *I know You're working.*

At the car, both men embraced, while Tom realized they had a new respect for one another.

Eurlene had trouble taking her eyes off Spencer. She thought she had sparked an interest with him. His amber eyes flecked with warmth. She found him both fascinating and breathtaking. She looked him over from head to toe. Licking her lips, she found him appealing. It surprised her that he was slipping through the cracks of her sealed heart.

After signing and receiving the papers, she gave a flirtsome wink to Spencer, but she quickly left the business table and hurried to catch Jud. Taking a deep breath, she yanked at Jud's arm. She let her eyes widen more than usual. "Will you take me back to the hospital? I need to see Karen."

The men arched their brows, looked at each other, and appeared not to know what to say or do. They shrugged their shoulders, nodded, and rode back in the car the way they came, taking Eurlene with them.

Upon arriving, she could feel the people staring as she walked by. She straightened her form-fitting skirt, gave a wiggle, checked her ruby-red lipstick and sauntered into Karen's room. She gave a nod to Kate and a circular finger motioning for her to leave. Kate gasped. Unfolding from the chair and leaving her grown daughter's room, she shook her head and huffed.

A sweet fragrance floated in the air. Karen opened her eyes.

Looking down, Eurlene in her sultry, husky voice spoke. "Hi, there. How are you feeling?"

Karen beamed her eyes to the voice. Her fiery eyes widened. "You are Eurlene." Karen's voice was strained. "How well your hair color actually suits you. Being a stylist I see your type. Why are you here?" Karen shifted in the bed. "Go ahead and talk. I make a good audience."

Eurlene drew near. "I'm so sorry about the way we've met." She dropped her head. "My, the things you must have heard." Patting Karen hand, she smiled. "I want to share some things with you."

Karen blinked. "Why."

Eurlene's fast-speaking drawl came spurting out. "Seeing me must have been a shock. It appears my presence has taken a serious toll on you." She paced back and forth then reached for Karen's hand again. "Sweetie, I need to talk with you about Jud and the past."

Karen withdrew her hand. "Why do I need to know anything more?"

Bending low for only Karen's ears to hear, she whispered. "I was young and fended for myself. I learned my body was more attractive to the boys and men than my brain." Eurlene sighed. "With the recent death of my mother and watching my father's grief, I felt all alone. The transfer to a new school was overwhelming. Being assigned to Jud was both a blessing and a curse. His kindness and moral background was new for me."

Eurlene laughed haughtily. "He was defiantly a challenge. He had the desires for a woman, but lacked experience. His work was rewarded by my knowledge. I miscounted the monthly schedule and found I was pregnant, but still, I was much too young and uneducated to birth a child. My dad would have disowned me."

She walked to the window and back. "Abortion was the only answer. Dad had come home and called the school, and I had to come home. I was scared. But I was surprised. Everything was packed in boxes and we were on the move, still again. I had three and a half hours before we left. I remembered seeing an advertisement for women having unspoken doctor needs. That dreadful call left me sterile."

Tears spilled as she continued. "Sadness and unhappiness did set in for awhile. It was just too much to face. A few weeks passed. No one noticed how sad and withdrawn I had become. Dad had a Bible on his nightstand. With its dust and all, I flipped through the pages and there it was: 1 Peter 5:7 ("Casting all your cares upon Him for He careth for you").

"Karen, I prayed as never before. Knowing nothing could be changed, I made an oath to accept my fate. I refused to remain unhappy. Counting my attributes, I realized how very intellectual I could be. I concentrated and chose to get ahead and have everything out of life. Getting a business degree became my reason for living. Being successful was one of my goals along with being in charge of a company. Making a pledge, I decided there was no time for any men. I would not allow one in my life after Jud. I refused to let a man interfere or slow me down."

Leaning over the bed once more, in a very cruelly low voice, she continued, "Karen, if you ever think you don't love Jud or have no need of him, call me. I won't toss him aside. I could change my mind very easily." With arched eyebrows, she squared her shoulders. "I would do it in a heart beat. Quickly."

Karen gasped. Then her eyes narrowed.

"Sorry to be like this, Karen, but in my book he's worth it. He's a keeper! I made mistakes and have run ever since. I never stopped or looked back. Be wise, Karen, and be careful with your decisions."

With a haughty laugh, and a hand-fluffing to her hair, she tossed her head. "Jud never loved me. He mistook lust for love. After all, I was his first, but he wasn't mine."

Eurlene squeezed Karen's hand and wished her and the baby well. "I pray you have only the best of luck." There was one last passing look between both women, one of better understanding, and in an instant Eurlene clicked her colorful spiked heels and stepped out of the room.

# 14

Karen felt a little sorry just then for Eurlene and sent words upward. She was somewhat ashamed of her own actions. She thoroughly realized the insecurity she had carried all these years. She knew the redhead's type. Their reasoning for success may differ, but through their pain, they usually sold out and became hard-invested workers.

They called themselves "self achievers."

Karen heard the *click, click, click* of a return in Eurlene's steps. Karen glanced her way. Snortingly, Eurlene explained she had hidden Karen's purse from Jud. She couldn't have him unduly distracted from their business. She had also placed Karen's purse back when they arrived at the house. "I waited until Jud was out of the car and walking toward the house! I thought you ought to know." Again shoulders squared, she tilted her head back. Eurlene slithered, click after click from the room.

Karen strained to listen as Ken and Sara spoke to Eurlene just outside the door.

Ken whispered, "When I went into the chapel, Eurlene was sharing with Jud, pointing to his heart and showing a new spirituality being lived within. Eurlene, is this so?"

The hall was silent.

Tom had called Eurlene a cab. The driver was parked and pacing while waiting for someone to come out. The meter was ticking. Eurlene touched Tom's cheek and breathed good-bye. Men glared and motioned for her. Adjusting her shoulders with head off-center, she pushed the revolving door leaving many unanswered questions. Unknowns only wished they had an opportunity to know a woman like her while they gawked, open-mouthed after her.

Donald gave a long sigh. They watched as she stepped into the cab. It was good to see the cab driver close her door, go around to his side, and fold himself behind the wheel. They waved, watching the smokey exhaust drift upward as the cab pulled away.

Donald looked at Tom and Jud. "I feel my heart rate slowing down." He had crinkles forming at the edge of his mouth. Tom knew a form of relief had settled in.

Karen watched Ken and Sara enter the room. Her voice cracked. "What a fool I've been! How did I get so off track? I don't know if Jud and I can ever mend our fences." Tears were threatening to spill.

Both Ken and Sara stepped to her bed. "Karen, it's not too late. Be open with Jud and communicate. He will meet you halfway. You can work out your issues. Seek divine help and then plead with Jud."

Sara tapped her foot and waved Ken out of the room. Karen could tell he was too familiar with that look. Adjusting his shoulders a sheepish smile came across his mouth as he calmly moved toward the door.

Karen spoke. "I need to see Jud for a minute." Ken stopped and turned. "I'll send Jud in. I'll be in the waiting room joining the others."

Before leaving, he patted Karen on the arm and whispered something in her ear. Karen noticed Sara watching as she tried to stifle a smile. Straightening up, he walked, bent down, and brushed Sara's lips. Whistling, he headed down the hall.

Karen ventured, "We're alone, friend." She motioned for Sara to speak. "I'm going to reminisce about the magical night I had with Ken, celebrating our anniversary." Karen heard something concerning the forgotten pill when an unwelcome pain stabbed her lower abdomen. She moaned.

"Help, help."

"What's wrong?"

"There's pain."

"Where?"

Karen shook her head and held up a hand. "I'm in too much misery to do any listening." She grabbed Sara's hand and squeezed hard.

"Karen, where do you hurt?"

She pointed at her stomach and pulled her legs upward. "Cramps and aches have begun."

Sara reached for the call light. Karen heard the ding as it was pressed. She was sure she heard Sara mumbling a prayer on her behalf.

"It's going to be all right, Karen."

Karen soon head quick, swift steps coming down the hall, and the nurse came in. Jud followed.

The nurse became very busy, bustling around, and insisted Karen needed more rest. She plumped and fluffed the pillows. She adjusted the bed and checked Karen's pulse. The nurse left to place a call to Doctor March. She returned with a light sedative administered in a drip flowing into Karen's arm.

Karen smelled Jud's aftershave and glanced to him, but caught the nurse motioning him to leave. Karen looked at Sara and heard everything was under control. Her eyes felt heavy as she glanced over her shoulder. "Karen, I'm going to leave now. It's Timmy's bedtime. I'll try and get back. Call me."

The nurse nodded her head as Sara lightly touched Karen's face again.

Karen's eyes fluttered once more as Sara slowly walked out of the room. She heard Ken's voice.

"Call me, my friend. Let us know if there is anything we can do. Keep us in the loop."

"I will, and thank you both for coming." Jud sighed. "They said she just needs quietness and bedrest."

All went quiet.

Seeing everything looked under control, Tom motioned for Jud. Placing a hand on his shoulder, they fell in step together. They walked wistfully down the hall. Viewing the cafeteria, they noticed very few people sitting. The rush had passed long ago. Both grabbed a cup of black coffee and a cold sandwich.

Tom looked sober at Jud and began to chat. "Jud, I know you're tired through and through."

Jud stretched and yawn.

"Dora and I want to know how Karen and the baby are doing, so you need to call!" He placed a hand on Jud's shoulder. "It's time for your old dad to get on the road and head home." There was a sigh. "You know it can get lonely, although it's been great to be a silent helper with you. I'm glad I'm retired."

As he gave Jud a bear hug and patted him on the back. Eye to eye, Tom offered some solid advice. "Jud, learn to be a listener. Be tender-hearted, kind, and fair. Use the fruit of the Spirit to guide you, and most of all, don't be afraid to show Karen you love her. Unconditionally!"

Tom and Jud, man to man, exchanged a few more comments and sentiments. Embracing each other once again with new understanding, they had found a new height in their respect for one another. Their brown-flecked and green-sparkled eyes held a purposeful look that said everything. Empathy and compassion had developed among them to a privileged relationship of a higher level as father and son.

Donald and Kate talked with Jud. "We've decided to stay a few days longer. Is it all right to stay at your home? It's just in case there is a need."

Jud hunched his shoulders, putting his hands in his pockets. "Sure and thanks. If you need me, I'll be at the hospital with Karen."

Jud had scheduled a time for Kate to come to the hospital. But she sniffled. "I'll get there when I get there. But it will be daily. Poor dear." She nodded to Jud and read to Karen. He noticed it seemed to have a soothing effect on Karen and her breathing remained calm.

Jud shook his head and was amused when Donald without Kate knowing, slipped a few vanilla milkshakes in to Karen. Jud watched Karen's face light up when he came. She was delighted and smiled with glee but would arch her brows and tried to seriously scold him. Jud was in the doorway when he heard Karen and Kate talking about the secret shakes her dad would bring. The three were mused and had a great time laughing at his expense.

Jud, realizing the need for Karen and him to have a fresh start, headed into her room. He had prayed and was ready to give a well-rehearsed speech. "Good morning, Karen, honey."

"Stop!"

There he stood with flowers again. Karen threw her hand up, beckoning for silence. Half sitting in the bed, she motioned him to come and sit.

Obeying, he dropped a kiss sheepishly on Karen's forehead and sat where she patted.

His strained words were almost breathlessly uttered. "Talk with me, Karen. Please."

Her jaw dropped. "Jud, I was wrong about us." Swallowing, he held his breath. "Karen, is it too late for us? Have I waited too long in telling you the truth?" Karen patted his hand and a tear dropped. "You know, I've turned you away at important times. Jud, it was because I was afraid. I didn't know how to share my thoughts or feelings." Tears fell.

Jud gently brushed her tears and held her close. "We can work through this, Karen. All I know is that I don't ever want to lose you." He took her soft limp hands in his. "I know you are my soul mate."

They locked eyes. "Jud, I need you to try and understand something. I was not brought up knowing anything about intimacy. It was not ever mentioned on what a person did or did not do. I didn't even know what one was to expect."

"Shush, shush. It's going to be all right."

She shook her head. "I realize my mother tried speaking with me, but the only information she offered was 'Karen, you will experience a moment of togetherness for yourself. Let him take the lead. Everything will come naturally. It's just the way of life.' I didn't understand. I thought I had to have certain nightwear for you to know what to do."

A smile crept at the corners of his mouth. Karen took his leathered, warm hand to her heart.

"Confessing is scary but also sacred." She looked into his eyes. "I love you." A burn was on her neck and reached her face.

Jud sat silently staring in disbelief. *She loves me.*

Chokingly, she whispered. "I need to know when and how to respond. Will you teach me?"

His face stained, Jud pulled her closer to him. "I promise." He dropped little kisses. "I will answer all your needs and what a pleasure." As he rose, a smoldering warmth came from his eyes. "You, my beloved, are a true blessing in disguise. You have been sent from heaven above and been given wholeheartedly to me."

Through stained faces they beamed. Both Jud and Karen were touched and thrilled at their newfound honesty between themselves. She kissed. He kissed. They hugged until Karen had trouble breathing. She placed a hand to his chest and looked into his wide eyes. *Huff, huff, huff.* "Call the nurse."

Jud pushed the call button and ran to the hall. "My wife needs help."

The nurse smiled while looking at Karen and Jud. She patted Karen's arm as she turned off the light. She glanced at the lights flashing off and on the monitor. The signals went crazy. They were all over the place. She barked. "Move, sir. Please get out of the way." She reached the phone and called for backup. The nurses' shoes squeaked as they came running down the hall and calling out codes.

Jud paced. "Help her."

Karen felt faint. Jud's face wavered before her. The doctor arrived. "Karen could go into labor at any time. It may be today, or it could be up to two, maybe three weeks. First time babies are tricky. We think we have her stable now."

The nurse wanted Karen moved closer to the nurse's station, where she could be better monitored. "Jud, it's only for precaution. We just wanted to keep an eye on Karen and the baby. It's for safety reasons."

The staff brought Jud in a chaise so he could relax and get some rest. But his feet hung over the end; and besides, the chaise was very lumpy, so no rest came. He was past being tired. He was running on fumes—low fuel, almost empty.

During the night Karen broke into a sweat. Jud came quickly to her side, asking her to take deep breaths.

In between the pains, she kept telling Jud of her love for him, over and over, as though he were going to vanish. He squeezed her hand and kept patting it. It gave him an unexpected energy. "I'm not going anywhere." He reached for her hand and tried to help steady her breathing again so she would be stable. Raking his hand through his hair, it appeared to him it was going to be a long two or three weeks lying ahead for the both of them.

He walked over to the window and looked up.

*Please be with her and the baby.*

The next day, Doctor March was making his late afternoon rounds. He stopped in Karen's room to check on her. With little observation, he said, "Girl, you're in labor."

Karen looked at him disbelievingly.

Jud looked at the doctor and back at Karen. "What?"

"I'm uncomfortable. Can I get up?"

The doctor shook his head. He had the nurse time Karen's labor pattern, and the pains were coming every five minutes, lasting up to a minute.

Jud, in disbelief, tried to soothe her. Observing her, he did not know how anyone could have so much pain. Karen listened, but she said she could not help much. "She's a natural."

"Let's get our staff in here!" Scrubbing his hands and bellowing out the orders, the nurse placed his gloves on. The equipment was placed to his left and switched on was the overhead light, ready for action.

The first push came. Beads of sweat broke out on Karen's forehead. Second push came.

The doctor said, "Karen you're doing fine. Relax in between. Breathe."

The third push came. This time it was harder and lasted longer. The fourth push came. Karen yelled.

Jud wiped her brow and placed a hand over hers. He gave her a pleading look and squeezed her hand. "You're awesome."

The fifth push came. The doctor exclaimed. "I see the baby. It's coming."

Karen bore down again, grunting and pushing. "It's a girl," the nurse said as she showed Karen and handed Jud their baby. The nurse helped Jud tilt the baby toward Karen.

He stood there mouth opened, looking back and forth at Karen and the baby. He beamed from ear to ear. He was amazed to see his daughter.

They announced, "She weighs five pounds and six ounces."

The doctor stated, "Jud, Karen and the baby are doing fine. The baby is small but defiantly healthy and pink! We are sending her to the nursery. It's just a precaution."

Someone screamed. They turned. It was Karen. She started the same huffing and puffing and began pushing again. Jud handed the baby back to the nurse to be placed in the incubator. Jerking his head around, he looked at the doctor. The doctor hunched his shoulders.

Getting into position, he said, "Karen, push, push, push."

She puffed, puffed, and puffed. Jud was puffing too. Sweat came down both Jud's and the doctor's brows. The nurse quickly wiped the forehead of the doctor. A half hour went by, then another. Karen looked pale. She repeated the huffing and puffing over and over, and it seemed like a very long time. Then there was a push and a shrill, unforgettable scream. Then the news came. Dr. March announced. "It's a baby boy. He's a little heavier, six pounds, one and one-half ounces." He glanced at Jud and Karen smiled. "You have twins."

# 15

Jud passed out. When he awoke lying in a hospital bed, he felt stunned and rather stupid. Thoughts overtook him. *What about being a he-man?* Jud did not feel very manly at the moment. The nurse smiled. "You're going to be all right,

Jud." She handed him orange juice. "Drink."

Sheepishly Jud accepted the cup. "Thanks." She touched his forehead. "Fainting happens more than men would like to admit. Your color is back. Your wife is in the same room."

Karen's eyes brightened when he walked into the room. "Where'd you go? What happened?'

The doctor nodded, and Jud changed the subject. "I see he's busy taking care of little ones."

The corners on Jud's mouth lifted until he was beaming. Bending, he kissed Karen. He urged her to get some much-needed rest. "You looked so radiant." Karen closed her eyes, waving Jud to the waiting room.

Jud took long strides and loudly announced to her parents, "Karen delivered twins: a girl and a boy, just in that order."

Donald smiled while pumping Jud's hand. He touched Donald's arm and removed the other hand from his. Kate dabbed her eyes then embraced Jud. They asked all the questions one would about babies. They nervously babbled on and on about the weight, how many inches long, if they had any hair, how many toes and fingers, and the like.

Jud's shirttail had come out. His sleeves were rolled up, and his slacks had a worn look.

"Want to see the babies?"

Nudging him side by side, they headed to the nursery. "Look." The babies had arrived. They were placed side by side looking at each other in the incubators.

The nurses were busy placing wrist bracelets on each baby. One was a porcelain bracelet with pink beading, spelling "Girl—Day." The other one was a porcelain bracelet done in blue, spelling out "Boy—Day."

They were under a heat lamp for they needed warmth for their new adjustment in the march of life to the world.

Jud watched Karen's parents take a peek at the new lives so preciously given from above. He laughed. The baby boy was out of the lower half of the blanket while the girl baby looked at peace with the world. All sighed.

The nurse placed name tags on each bed. Donald spoke. "Jud, Kate and I are going to make a few phone calls."

Jud raised his shoulders. "I need to do that, also." Donald, Kate, and Jud hurriedly went and used the hospital phones to share the joyful news.

Jud called Ken and basked in the news. After hanging up, Jud bowed his head. *Thanks for listening and caring.* A tear dropped.

The phone was ringing. No one answered, so he left a brief message for his dad about the twins on the answering machine. He called his mother, but again, there was no answer. He couldn't leave a message for the machine was full. He rubbed his chin. "I'll call her shortly."

The three stepped into the room to congratulated Karen. The nurse huffily raised a hand and shooed them out. "Go home. Come back later. She's going to rest."

Karen raised both her hands and flopped back into the bed.

After five days, Karen was able to leave the hospital, feeling much rested. The twins were dressed in their tiny outfits brought in by Jud. Karen, with the nurse, dressed the baby boy first for he was not one to be kept waiting. A little white sleeper trimmed in blue was placed on him. It tied at the bottom to keep his feet in. The little girl was dressed in a pink sleeper, also with the hem tied to keep her feet warm. Both were wrapped in their special blankets made by Timmy's grandma, Louise.

What an exciting day. Jud sought to help them. "Here do you need this?" He held up a little pair of blue socks.

Karen snatched them. "Move." She smiled at him. Jud handed the release papers for the twins and Karen to the nurse. She seated Karen in the wheelchair and handed the twins to her, placing one in each of her arms. Karen rested back in the seat with a contented sigh. Everything was perfect.

Kate fussed around, phoning the department store to get another completed set of coverings and white bassinet. The store obliged and the owner made a special trip. The bassinet arrived just in the nick of time. Donald signed for them.

"Donald, help me get this set up. Jud is in the driveway."

Now they had a layette for the girl in pink and one for the boy in blue. Kate was all jabbers while the babies were placed.

The following week Donald and Kate helped while Jud and Karen attempted to get adjusted in being a family of four. Just trying to juggle or have a schedule was something else. Jud would heat a bottle. Karen would feed. The other twin cried. Kate held the baby while Jud fixed another bottle. She would hand baby 2 over in Karen's arms, also. The feeding of both the twins was something to behold. Diaper changes seemed like there was no end in store. Bathing at first was awful. After two days into it, the twins had settled down in the water. Seeking a sleep pattern at times seemed nearly impossible.

Jud scheduled a month's leave from work to help and bond with the twins.

Ken, being expertly trained by Jud, made a great relief person at the bank. He was glad for the event, knowing he could step up to the plate. Being both friends and coworkers with Jud didn't hurt anything either. It was a plus for they knew how to relate business with one another and just talk. A new offer in banking came through telegraph: *New bank-Mississippi. Need CPO to operate and manage location. Will help with relocating fees.* Ken scratched his chin. Wow. Ken called Jud with the news.

"Sounds good, Ken. Like it could be a great opportunity. We'll talk more when I return."

A month had nearly passed. Kate and Donald's visit came to a close. Over breakfast, they told Karen and Jud. "Day after tomorrow our fight leaves."

Jud was a little choked. "You are both such a huge help mentally, physically, and spiritually. 'Thanks' is such a small word to say."

Karen heard the twins and went to check on them.

Jud reached over to Kate and looked at Donald. "Will you watch the twins tomorrow? I would like to make plans to take Karen out for her birthday. Just her and me."

Donald and Kate looked at each other. Donald reached for a refill of coffee. "Jud we have agreed to watch the twins. It will be our pleasure." Kate, hands in her lap, smiled.

Early the next day after the twins were down, Jud led Karen to the car. As they were walking, he paused and dropped her a kiss. At the car, he seated Karen. He was folding into the driver's seat when Donald came rushing out. "Wait. Here's a birthday card from your mother and me." He broadened his smile as she reached out the window with her hand. It was for her twenty-sixth birthday.

Karen stepped from the car and gave him a hug. Her eyes flashed happiness. "Thank you both. You've already have done so much."

He flushed pink. "Go on now."

Jud had come around as Karen looked to him. "We have come so far. How silly it was to keep secrets."

Jud squirmed but squeezed her hand and lowered his head and brushed her lips.

Looking into Jud's eyes before sliding across the seat only confirmed the passion they had discovered between themselves. His eyes were twinkling.

"Karen, we have the whole day together alone. Can you believe it?"

Karen reddened. She gave him a wink.

They had been driving for about forty-five minutes. "Wonder how the twins are?"

Jud mused. "Your mom and dad sure seem happy to spend time at home with them."

"Silly, it's their grandchildren."

"Should we call?"

"They'll be fine. Now scoot over here." Jud smiled wickedly. As the car turned in the drive, he said, "Surprise!"

Karen clasped her hands. "This place! Oh, Jud, it's so expensive. I'm delighted though."

The restaurant was bright and cheerful and hidden in a cliff off the country road. The sign read, "Special: Fried Chicken all you can eat."

Jud's mouth began to water. He wiped it to make sure he wasn't drooling. Karen's stomach rumbled and then growled. Both wanted the chicken meal so Jud ordered two country chicken dinners.

The waitress brought two gigantic pieces of chicken, mashed potatoes, gravy, green beans, and four biscuits. "That's for starters. Let me know when you want more." She turned and disappeared.

Jud motioned for the waitress and ordered dessert. They didn't speak while the she cleared the table. Music was playing, and Jud reached for Karen's hand. "Feel like dancing?"

Karen's eyes fluttered. "Who wants to know?" His wicked smiled returned. He led her to the dance floor and kept a close hand on her back as they waltzed.

He noticed the waiter had come with his apple pie and it was loaded with ice cream served on top. Also, the waiter sat Karen's piece of steaming peach cobbler down. Hand in hand they walked to the table. A happy quietness had settled as they ate until they were both stuffed.

Sipping her tea, she opened the card from her parents. It was so sweet. But inside there was a note which stated, "At the town bank, we your parents, have deposited your dowry. The amount shown in the account is twenty-six thousand dollars." She sat there with her mouth open.

Jud positioned his arm around her. "Hey, what's with the surprised look?"

A nervous laugh began. It bubbled as she turned to Jud. Karen lifted her hand out to Jud. "Here, take a look."

Jud, with an arm around Karen, looked at her in unbelief. "You have any idea how you are going to use the money?" He hunched his shoulders. "That's the banker in me."

"I'm not sure. I think I'll let it stay in the account for now and collect interest. We need to pray about this. Then we'll talk."

He nodded his head. "Agreed. Good plan." He touched her face, bent, and gave her a kiss.

Jud left the money for the bill and a good-sized tip on the table. As Jud seated Karen in the car, he was smiling at her. She noticed while he was driving a deep dimple appeared on the right side of his face. *Wonder if he's hiding something?* He looked so relaxed and how magnificently rugged he was. *Handsome and he's mine.* She opened her mouth and saw they were parking out in front of her childhood home.

Being puzzled, she asked, "What…Why are we here?"

"I knew you wanted to see the old place again, so here we are."

Karen just beamed. "How did you know? Thanks." She clapped her hands. "It's good to see the old homestead again." Looking around the yard, she took it all in. "The 'for sale' sign has been replaced. It says, 'sold.'" A humble sadness gripped her. She let out a forlorn sigh.

Jud took her hand as he opened the car door. As they walked, she saw Nathan standing on the front porch of the house. It appeared he had been waiting quite awhile for he was pacing.

"Nothing like being on time." Nathan unlocked and sprung the door. He stepped to the right so Karen and Jud could enter. She took three steps holding onto Jud. Karen stopped quickly for there on the living room floor were the boxes her mom had at the house.

She squeezed his hand. Glancing around at the windows, she saw the new draperies and knew her mother's finished work. She shook her head. She did not know how or when her mother had the time to do all that sewing. "Jud, look at the drapes. See their elegance and the way they are free-flowing. Mom never hurried these. They're just perfect. Someone will be very happy."

The flooded memories caused a blank look and a single tear to slip down Karen's cheek. Jud circled his arm around her shoulder and embraced to comfort her. He gently gave her a light kiss on top of her head.

Karen saw Jud's tense face and knew he was holding back. She felt so vulnerable as her knees gave way when he touched her. Karen bit the inside of her cheek and saw he had bitten his lip. Her stomach churned and ached.

They couldn't keep their hands off of each other. She touched his hands as he reached for the buttons on her blouse and slid his hand in. She withdrew and tilted her head. "We have to wait."

"How long?"

She blushed then giggled. "Two weeks."

He stepped back and grabbed her hand. The twinkling of their eyes only reconfirmed their love and deep desire for one another.

On the tip of her toes she gave him a smoky kiss. Karen mentioned hoarsely, "Let's go to the basement and take a look."

"Lead the way." He jiggled his slacks.

# 16

This time, she was determined and carried a flashlight and a damp cloth. It was one of Jud's old handkerchiefs, which he had volunteered.

Slowly, she went down the steep stairs with Jud closely behind her. Karen picked up the pillow and carried it to kneel down on by the drain. She vigorously began cleaning the viewing glass on top of the big drain plug.

She glanced at Jud and he was staring with his brows extensity arched. As she dared to look, gasping, she placed both hands on the viewer. She looked at Jud then back to the viewer. A giggle slipped out. Sitting there, more laughter began. "Jud, come and look!"

Rising up, she motioned for him to hurry.

Jud knelt and placed his hands on the viewer. Being all excited and with glancing eyes searching hers, he let out a breath. "Wow! I can't believe there's water running below the basement floor." Then he became speechless.

Karen stretched her arms. "It's a natural spring. Now we both know my childhood secret of the house."

Jud wanted to know more. He had all kind of questions, but he could not wait any longer to share the birthday gift he had gotten for her.

Jud, being sober, stood and raised a hand to Karen's shoulder and, with the other hand, pulled an envelope out from his jacket inside pocket touching her nose. "Karen, please, we must never let any more secrets come between us from this day forward."

She nodded, but he caught her blushing. She looked like a child standing there. "Can I open it now?"

"Sure. Need any help?"

Shaking her head, she carefully began opening up the fat envelope making sure nothing was torn. When it was open, she pulled out a form, looking from top to bottom. "It looks like something legal."

"It's a deed." She hurriedly looked and read the papers out loud. "It's to the homestead house." She clasped the deed to her heart. "It's to my homestead house."

Jud viewed the surprise sparkle in her eyes and saw the flat line of her mouth turn to a crinkle. Elated, he swung her around. He slowly let her down, but Karen turned, jumped, and hung on tight. She wrapped her arms around his neck, and her legs encircled his waist. He felt her warmth and heard her excitement.

"I'm so happy. She nuzzled her head on his shoulder. "Thank you, Jud."

Karen started crying uncontrollably and shook. Being ever so attentive, he cuddled her in his bulging arms, rocking her back and forth. She at last knew he had proclaimed his love for her. She cuddled closer and felt secure and so fully loved, and very complete.

Karen gave a contented sigh. *Sometimes you do not need words between each other to speak, for actions speak for themselves. It makes sense.*

Having the deed for the old homestead house had been a life-long dream of hers. She secretly had wished to buy it but never really expected an action on it.

Silently, she took his hand and carefully climbed the stairs, step by step. Both noticed Nathan had left, but not before removing the realty sign. He had taken it from the front yard. Lying on the kitchen counter, they found his little note of thanks and congratulations on the purchase of their first house. He wished them happiness for their twins.

Karen reached for Jud's arm while leaning into him. On her toes, she stretched to touch his lips. Seeming to obey the urge, he lowered his lips to claim hers in a tender, gentle kiss. Karen looked up and a rush of passion was felt. They kissed, and their lips were swollen and sore. Their eyes spoke, promising the other there was more to come. Wickedly, Karen whispered, "Jud, the doctor indicated we only have to wait two more weeks."

She undoubtedly knew his hardness had set in. They felt fireworks exchange between them. It was a new experience. They spoke to each other. "Karen, I have never had such feelings or desire with anyone before."

"Nor I, Jud."

They let out a long breath.

"You said two weeks? Oh, that seems so far away."

"I know."

Shaking, she had felt the heat and knew without doubt what she was to do.

She took his hand and guided him toward the stairs. They edged their way slowly, downstairs one more time, where she turned to the viewing glass on top of the big storm drain. Eagerly she took his hand. "My father especially designed this part of the basement. He had the house built over this body of water.

Holding Karen's hand he faced her. "What did you say?"

"In 1945, my father and mother drew up the plans for this house. But my dad planned the basement. The water is called a spring. Its flow channels a steady current under this spot. Daddy built Mom this private indoor pool for her enjoyment and for their child or children thereafter." She shook her head. "Poor Mom, her sinuses were so badly infected after using the pool. She eventually required a doctor's care until recently.

Karen explained that the doctor told her dad that the basement held a lot of humidity from the body of water. There was no water treatment and system to help her not get infected when she was around the water.

"Jud, it was awful to see my father that way. Dad, without any hesitation, said as his fist hit the table at the doctor's office, 'I will not see her suffer. I will close it up and seal it. There will be no more pool. It was meant for fun and relaxation, not this living nightmare!'"

Karen sighed. "Mom touched Dad on his chest and tried to plead with him, knowing of her love for it and the expense he had poured into the development of the pool. The shape of the floor and walls were built around the spring. But within a forty-eight hour period, he had arranged for the spring to be plugged, and it remained closed, you know, even until this day. I was about ten years old when it was sealed. It was never to be spoken of again."

"Oh, Jud, the secret of the house has lain beneath the plug with the viewing glass until now. If you had not bought this house only I would have known, and the secret would have gone to my grave."

Jud squeezed her hand. "Why did you want to know if the spring was still here? Would you like to have the pool reopened?"

Karen snuggled closer. "Oh, yes. The doctor has given me a clean bill of health. No sinusitis."

He hugged her and seemed caught up in her happiness. "I will consult your dad and get his input and information. Karen, when I was in another state I witnessed a new system that's out. It uses salt, although it's only in the trial testing stages. They have reported good usage as of today."

She clasped her hands and nodded out of true delight. Jud went on talking about calling in an engineer and architect. She agreed by nodding her head.

"We can open and try to recreate the pool as much as possible."

They walked a short distance. "I wouldn't think it would require much work. What do you think?" She hunched her shoulders. "I certainly hope not. We have the funds." Karen scrunched her nose. "Jud, tell me more about the product, the salt and how it could be used. I know salt is a healer, and it is pure. Maybe if salt could be used, it would sanitize and maybe no harsh chemicals would be needed." Jud placed his hand under his chin. "Yes, it would be nice to use natural chemicals."

"You know the heat from the original design kept the pool's water well-tempered all year round. The cement floors have another kind of special heating.

Jud saw a water test kit hung on the wall. *Wonder if it would still be good.*

"Karen, if I tap the viewer open, will the water gush in?"

"No. The drain plug has to come up. There's a built in safety vale. Why?"

In his hand, he had a strip, and he reached for a sample of pool water. Karen placed her hands at her mouth and gasped. The spring water tested pure.

"Of course, we'll try new strips and we will keep our spring pure." His eyes danced.

Jud folded his arms across his chest.

"Jud, I want you to have free reign of my money to use from the dowry my parents gave me. "What a birthday."

Jud looked seriously at her. "We'll pray and do this project side by side, decision by decision. Yes, a new makeover."

Both agreed the professionals would need to be called so the spring would be brought up to code when finished, and before moving into the house.

As they walked upstairs Jud touched her white gold necklace with the lighthouse charm on it, and it sent a new electric awakening through him. Karen reached for his hand while winking. He beamed a lopsided grin.

Hand in hand through their house, they talked and planned out every room and its reconstruction.

They glanced at each other and eyes locked their facial expressions which showed a commitment. Karen whispered, "We came so close to losing everything valuable in life."

She gave a light kiss and breathed heavily. "Yes, too close."

Silently they nodded and quietly renewed their vows.

*He knows our secrets. He hears and answers.*

Then they both paused. "Karen, this house feels like home. It's good and right."

Before leaving, with one last look, they took in what would be their master bedroom, making oohs and ahhs. Jud, taking her in his arms and holding her close again said, "Woman, it will be hard to wait." Thrills and chills ran down Karen's spine at his promises. She shivered.

She quickened her steps as she walked toward the twins' bedroom. Jud pointed. "This one could be decorated really special."

Karen noticed it was the room across the hallway to the left. "Let's call it, The Bay, like on Lake Erie." Down the hall and at an angle to the right, she gestured. "This would be the other twin's bedroom."

He nodded. "Would it be called, The White Sands, as it was when we were on the beach?" Jud sucked in his cheeks, but a laugh escaped.

Karen optimistically jumped and clapped her hands. "Let's get Sara to design their rooms for us! Think she will?"

He put his hands in his pocket, and creases formed at his mouth as it turned up. A chuckled slipped out and surprised him. He saw her mind working with the wheels in motion. Looks of admiration fell on her face. "Jud, the twins, Luke and Luci, are so much loved, and definitely, they will be very enchanted here! There's lots of room."

"Karen," Jud whispered as he very tenderly but firmly pulled her into his arms. Eye flecks of passions flowed between them. "We all will surely embark on a new beginning of honesty, and it will be real. There's no room for any secrecies or lack of communication between us anymore. Not with us in the march of life."

Karen beheld his bright clear green eyes and placed a hand to his chest. "Jud, you have gained my trust, and I adore you. I now know it was there all the time." She crossed her fingers behind her back. Her eyes sparkled. "I promise no more secrets." *Except birthdays and special grown-up times.*

"I love you Karen and with my whole heart." Jud smiled. "I knew how I felt when we first met at the Wednesday night reading group." Kissing her nose, he laughed. "You know what?"

She looked up. "What?"

"I always will be hopelessly in love with you." Karen smiled and rocked back and forth on her feet.

As they turned to leave, she saw that look in his eyes and saw his stern jaw. She knew they had faced their worst fears and foes, and for a brief moment, she let out a slow sigh and closed her eyes. Scripture came to mind. *For there is nothing hid, which should not be manifested; neither was any thing kept secret, but that it should come abroad.* Her eyes went wide as she thought. *I need to tell Jud about this verse. Maybe this can become our key verse.*

Karen was brought back to reality as his warm breath and wood smell blew across her face. His lips touched her cheek ever so gentle. She glanced and blinked. Her eyes open wide. Had she dreamed this or was standing there with Jud real? Karen stroked his face and seeing his smoldering green eyes darken she knew reality and they had surely crossed the threshold into a promise of the march of life.

"Jud?"

"What darling?" He looked at her soberly.

She stood with an index finger tapping at the side of her head. "Um, Jud, I think I'll call the doctor tomorrow."

He broke into a wicked grin, showing dimples, and his brows shot up. Jud lifted her to him, bent and gave her a warm, passionate commitment kiss. Setting her down, he still encircled her. "Karen, you promise?"